U0084677

序　言

　　在國際交流日益頻繁的今天，無論是觀光旅遊、參加會議、或出國唸書進入新班級，都有可能被要求做**自我介紹**。因爲在一個陌生的團體聚會中，自我介紹是讓人彼此認識的最有效方法，同時也可由此展開個別的談話。所以學習如何自我介紹，尤其是用英文做自我介紹，絕對有其必要。

　　本書共分四章，第一章列舉各種場合的自我介紹，是模擬練習的絕佳範例。第二章則歸納出一篇自我介紹可能包含的基本項目與實用例句，並加以各種句型的變換，可供讀者充分活用。相信您看完第二章後再翻閱前章，必有駕輕就熟之感。

　　本書三、四章的編寫是針對私下交談，或活動進行中所展開的進一步自我介紹。尤其是第三章，特別介紹談話應注意的事項及其相關技巧，可奠定會話成功的基礎。第四章則分四大類 72 項，列出與自己有關的各種談話題材，以供進一步的交談。其中每項並以對話形式先舉出三個例子，來幫助讀者練習提出、或回答問題。

　　爲何把重點放在自己呢？這是因爲各種流行話題可能隨時而變，唯有關於自己的資料，才最好掌握；而且表達自己，交換對彼此的詢問，要比談論政治、經濟等更能增加親密感。最後希望經由本書，您能從自我介紹開始，增進自己與外籍人士交往的信心，並因而促進成功的國民外交。

編者　謹識

目　錄

附錄

第一章 各種場合的自我介紹

1 參加聯誼活動的自我介紹

(1)

> *Good morning, ladies and gentlemen. I am July Yang. I come from Taiwan, the Republic of China*, and I am currently a student at USC. My favorite pastime is listening to music, especially classical music. I am majoring in educational psychology and hope to be a teacher in the future.
>
> *I am so glad I could be with you today. I hope everybody has a good time. Thank you.*

　　早安，各位先生，各位女士。我是楊茱麗。我來自中華民國台灣。我目前是南加大的學生。我最喜歡的消遣是聽音樂，尤其是古典音樂。我主修教育心理學，希望將來能當老師。

　　今天很高興和大家在一起，祝大家愉快，謝謝。

* pastime〔'pæs,taɪm,'pɑs-〕*n.* 消遣
  major〔'medʒɚ〕*v.* 主修
  classical〔'klæsɪk!〕*adj.* 古典的
  psychology〔saɪ'kɑlədʒɪ〕*n.* 心理學

參加聯誼活動的自我介紹(2)

Good morning. My name is Ai-ch'in Yuan. My family consists of my father, mother and myself. I am nineteen years old. At present I am studying at the National Taiwan University, majoring in politics. My ambition is to be a diplomat and to do some useful things for my country. My hobbies are reading books and traveling, which I find very interesting. I can drive a car and also enjoy playing the piano. Since I am the only child in my family, I am quite independent and now I can support myself. I deeply believe that I can succeed in the future.

早安，我叫袁愛琴。我家有三個人，父親、母親和我。我今年十九歲，現就讀於國立台灣大學，主修政治。我的抱負是成為一個外交家並為國家做一些有益的事。我的嗜好是讀書和旅行，這些都帶給我許多樂趣。我會開車也愛彈鋼琴。由於我是家裏的獨子，所以我很獨立，而且現在我也能負擔我自己的生活。我深信我將來能成功。

* *consist of* 由～組成
  at present 目前
  diplomat〔ˈdɪpləˌmæt〕*n.* 外交家

參加聯誼活動的自我介紹(3)

Good morning, ***everybody***. My name is Wei-ru Ch'en. I am twenty years old, an English major, and live in Taipei.

I've always been a curious person and enjoy many things, in particular, music and reading. I am the eldest child in my family, and I have three brothers and sisters.

I really enjoy my life now — being a student and allowing my curiosity to guide me to know more and more of what is yet unknown to me.

大家早，我叫陳威如，二十歲，外文系學生，住在台北。

我一直都是很好奇的人，喜歡的東西很多，尤其是音樂和閱讀。在家中我排行老大，下有三個弟妹。

我很喜歡目前的生活——做一個學生，讓好奇心帶領我逐漸地去瞭解我所不瞭解的事。

* major〔'medʒɚ〕*n.* 主修的學生〔課程〕
appreciate〔ə'priʃɪˌet〕*v.* 欣賞
unknown〔ʌn'non〕*adj.* 未知的

參加聯誼活動的自我介紹(4)

Good afternoon, fellow students.　My name is
Shu-chuan Huang.　I come from Taiwan.　I am majoring in English at the Chinese Culture University
now.　There are five people in my family, including my
father, mother, two brothers and myself.　Having
been deeply influenced by my family, I love clean-
liness very much.

　　I am the kind of person who is easily moved and
somewhat of a perfectionist, even in small things.
But I know that I do need more self-confidence to see a
thing through to the finish.　Though I have many
interests, English is what I like most.　I want
to keep on learning new things to increase my
ability and broaden my horizons.

　　午安，同學們。我叫黃淑娟，來自台灣，目前在中國文化大學主修
英文。我家有五個人，包括我父親、母親、二個哥哥和我。我深受家庭
影響，非常愛乾淨。

　　我是個易受感動的人，而且有點完美主義，即使是小事也不放過。
但是我知道我的確需要更多自信心來完成一件事。我雖然有很多興趣，
英文卻是我最喜歡的。我要不斷學習新的東西來增進我的能力，並擴展
我的視野。

2 參加觀光團體的自我介紹

(1)

Hi, everybody. I am David Lin. I come from Free China and I run a Chinese restaurant in New York. I am so happy to have had the chance to visit this city. New York is a wonderful city and now I have found San Francisco is also a charming city. It is so warm and comfortable. Perhaps a David Restaurant will be built here one day.

My son in college said that he wants to be an excellent cook in the future. However, I hope my son does not become a cook like me, for my wife is always on a diet. *Thank you.*

嗨，大家好。我是林大衞，我來自自由中國，在紐約經營一家中國餐館。我很高興有機會遊覽這個城市，紐約是個美妙的都市，而我現在發現舊金山也是個迷人的地方。它是這麼暖和，這麼舒服，也許將來這裏會蓋一家大衞餐廳。

我唸大學的兒子說他將來想當一個優秀的廚師，不過我希望我兒子不要成爲一個像我一樣的廚師，因爲我太太一直在節食。謝謝。

參加觀光團體的自我介紹(2)

Good morning, everybody. I am Danny Chou. I come from Taiwan. and I am still a student in high school. In school I am interested in biology, especially in animals. So *I am very glad to be able to visit Yellowstone National Park*. I've been told that it is famous for its bears. So I hope that if anyone is fortunate enough to see a bear, I hope he will inform me before hurrying for a safe shelter. *Thank you.*

大家早，我是周丹妮。我來自台灣，我還是一個中學生。在學校裏，我對生物，尤其是動物很感興趣，所以我很高興能夠來遊覽黃石國家公園。人家說黃石公園以熊聞名，所以我希望如果有人幸運地看到熊，他能在急著找安全避難所之前先通知我。謝謝。

* biology〔baɪˈɑlədʒɪ〕*n.* 生物學
  inform〔ɪnˈfɔrm〕*v.* 通知
  shelter〔ˈʃɛltɚ〕*n.* 避難所

參加觀光團體的自我介紹(3)

Good morning, everybody. My name is Vicky Yang. I come from Taiwan. I am a student at Davis University, and I am majoring in mass communication. *I'm glad to come with you to visit this beautiful town.*

I know all of you are students from various schools in different states and majoring in various subjects. I am sure we can share much knowledge with each other. *Maybe we'll become good friends. Have a good time ! Thank you.*

大家早。我叫楊維琪，來自台灣。我是戴維斯大學的學生，主修大衆傳播。我很高興和你們拜訪這個美麗的城鎮。

我知道你們都是來自不同州的不同學校學生，而且主修不同的學科。我相信我們可以彼此分享很多見聞，也許我們會成爲好朋友。祝大家愉快！謝謝。

* mass communication 大衆傳播
 various〔ˈvɛrɪəs〕*adj.* 不同的；種種的

3 參加參觀活動的自我介紹

(1)

Good morning, everyone. I am Chien-hsun Ch'en. I come from Taiwan. I am a medical student from National Yang Ming Medical College. *I am glad to visit this famous American hospital.*

Though I still don't know much about medicine, I am surprised to see the advanced equipment of the hospital. It appears to be up to world standards.

By the way, I hope I can see more surgical instruments because I am very interested in surgery. *Thank you for your hospitality.*

大家早，我是陳建勳。我來自台灣，我是國立陽明醫學院的學生，我很高興來參觀這所美國有名的醫院。

雖然我對醫學懂得還不多，但是看到這家醫院進步的設備，我還是感到很驚訝。它顯然達到了世界水準。

對了，我希望我能參觀更多外科儀器，因為我對外科很感興趣。謝謝你們的招待。

參加參觀活動的自我介紹(2)

Good evening. My name is Shu-ling Chang, and I am from Taiwan. I am now working for a trading company, which sent me here to America to get further training. My hobbies are listening to music and reading books and magazines, especially those dealing with business and economics, which helps me a lot in my work, too.

I've found that our schedule is quite tight, and I think it means that there will be many places to see and many things to learn. So I hope I can do further research with you and exchange what I have gained with you.

晚安。我叫張淑凌，來自台灣。我現在在一家貿易公司工作，公司派我來美國這裏受進一步的訓練。我的嗜好是聽音樂、看書和雜誌，尤其是有關商業和經濟方面的，而這也對我的工作幫助不少。

我發現我們的行程很緊湊，我想這表示要看的地方很多，要學的地方也很多，所以我希望我能和你們多做研究，交換彼此的心得，謝謝。

4 參加會議的自我介紹

(1)

Good morning, ladies and gentlemen. I feel very honored to participate in this conference and shall begin by introducing myself. My name is Jim Yang. I come from Taiwan, the Republic of China, and am an officer of the Chinese Ministry of Foreign Affairs. *I have come here hoping to fulfil the following three purposes* :

First, I hope I can understand more about the culture of other countries. Of course I will also introduce my country to you if you would like.

Second, I would like to exchange opinions with you. I believe that that can benefit us a lot. *Third*, and this is the most important, I am hoping that all of us can bring the achievements of this conference back to each of our home countries, and make relations between our countries steadier. *Finally, I hope everything will go well. Thank you.*

　　早安，各位先生，各位女士。我感到非常榮幸參加這次會議，並將先從自我介紹開始。我叫楊吉姆，來自中華民國台灣，是中國外交部的官員，來到這裏我希望能達成三個目的：首先，我希望能多了解一下其他國家的文化，而當然如果你們喜歡，我也會把我的國家介紹給你們。第二，我想要和你們交換一些意見，我相信這將使我受益良多。第三，這也是最重要的，我希望我們都能把這次會議的成果帶回到每個人的國家，而使我們國家間的關係更穩固。最後，我希望一切進行順利。謝謝。

* honor〔ˈɑnɚ〕*v.* 給予～光榮
　　participate in 參加
　　ministry〔ˈmɪnɪstrɪ〕*n.*（政府的）部
　　fulfil(l)〔fʊlˈfɪl〕*v.* 完成
　　exchange〔ɪksˈtʃendʒ〕*v.* 交換
　　benefit〔ˈbɛnəfɪt〕*v.* 獲益
　　achievement〔əˈtʃivmənt〕*n.* 成就

參加會議的自我介紹(2)

Good afternoon, ladies and gentlemen. My name is Daisy Wang. I am a professor of English literature in Taiwan University. *I am very glad to have this chance to study modern English literature.*

English literature is not an easy subject. Many Chinese students have taken it, but only a few have been successful. I think having a bad foundation is undoubtedly a major reason for this. I hope this discussion will give me some new methods I can use to teach my students ways to learn English literature. *Thank you.*

午安，各位先生、女士。我叫王黛西，我是台大英國文學教授，我很高興有機會來研究當代英國文學。

英國文學不是一門簡單的課，許多中國學生都修這個課，但只有少數人唸得好。我想基礎不好無疑是主要的原因。我希望這次討論會提供我一些新的方法來教學生如何學習英國文學。謝謝。

* foundation〔faʊnˈdeʃən〕*n.* 基礎
  undoubtedly〔ʌnˈdaʊtɪdlɪ〕*adv.* 無疑地

5 接受面談的自我介紹

(1)

Good morning. My name is Jessica. I am a graduate of Chengchi University. I majored in English Literature. As an English major, I've more chances to practice English. I do love this language and hope to find a job in which I can use English. Also, I've taken some courses in economics and business administration. *If I am lucky enough to be accepted by your company, I am sure it will be the best position for me to make use of what I've learned.* I know trading companies have become more and more competitive here, and a job requiring responsibility is a good challenge to me. To be sure, there are many things I must learn in this trade. But if there is a chance, I would be glad to take it. *Thank you very much* !

　　早安。我叫潔西卡，畢業於政治大學，主修英文。由於專攻英文的關係，使我有更多的機會說英語。我很喜歡這個語言，希望可以找到一個能用英語的工作。我也修過一些有關經濟及企業管理的課程，如果有幸被錄用，我相信這將是一個最能發揮所學的工作。我知道這裏的貿易公司競爭越來越激烈，而一個要求有責任感的工作，對我而言將是一項絕佳的挑戰。當然在這行我要學的地方很多，但是如果有機會的話，我會很樂意學習的。謝謝！

* economics〔͵ikə'nɑmɪks,͵ɛk-〕 *n.* 經濟學
 business administration 企業管理
 make use of 利用
 trading〔'tredɪŋ〕 *n.* 貿易　　～company 貿易公司
 competitive〔kəm'pɛtətɪv〕 *adj.* 競爭性的
 responsibility〔rɪ͵spɑnsə'bɪlətɪ〕 *n.* 責任
 trade〔tred〕 *n.* 行業

接受面談的自我介紹(2)

Good afternoon. I am Sheng-chin Hsu. I graduated from the Department of Business Administration in Chung Hsing University.

Although I did not major in computer science in college, I was much attracted by the use of a computer. So, after my graduation, I went abroad to the University of Chicago to study computer science for two years to take a master's in computer science.

NEC is famous in Taiwan, especially its computer company. So it will be my honor to work here. Of course, it will also be challenging for me to train myself to apply what I've learned so far.

I hope I have a chance to develop my interests and capabilities here. Thank you.

午安。我叫許勝欽，畢業於中興大學企管系。

我在大學雖然不是主修電腦，但卻對電腦的用途深感興趣，所以我畢業後就出國到芝加哥大學唸了兩年的電子科學，並拿到了電腦碩士。

NEC在台灣很有名，尤其是它的電腦公司，所以能到這裏工作將是我的榮幸。而當然，能訓練自己將至今所學的加以應用，對我也具有挑戰性。

我希望我能有機會在這裏發展我的興趣與能力。謝謝。

6 新生自我介紹

(1)

Hello, everybody. My name is Ch'in Wang. I come from Taiwan, the Republic of China. *I am very happy to come here to study with you*. When I arrived at this school three days ago, I fell in love with it. It is so nice and beautiful, and everyone is kind to me. This school feels just like one big family to me.

I'm interested in sports, music and mountain-climbing. I also enjoy playing piano. I would love to play for you some time. *I hope I can become your friend soon*. *Thank you*.

哈囉，各位。我的名字叫王琴，我來自中華民國，台灣，我很高興來這裏和你們一起唸書。當我三天前來到這所學校時，我愛上了它。它是那麼好，那麼美，而每一個人對我也很親切。我感到這學校對我來說就像是一個大家庭。

我對運動、音樂和爬山很有興趣，也喜歡彈鋼琴，並樂意將來爲你們彈奏一曲。最後，我希望我能很快成爲你們的朋友。謝謝。

新生自我介紹(2)

Hi, everybody, I'm Jenny Ch'en. Taiwan, the Republic of China is my home. It's a beautiful place. You are welcome to pay a visit to her. If possible I will be your guide.

This is the first time I have come here to study. Everything here is new to me and I'm really impressed with its spirit of initiative. *I hope I can become accustomed to it soon with your kind help and be friends with you.*

When I was in college I liked walking around the beautiful campus talking with my friends. I am hoping that when we have time I can relive those happy memories here with you. Thank you.

嗨，各位，我是陳珍妮。中華民國台灣是我的家，那是個美麗的地方，歡迎你們來。如果可以的話，我會做你們的嚮導。

　　這是我第一次到這裏來唸書，這裏的每樣東西對我來說都是新的，而我也深深感受到它進取的精神。我希望經由你們親切的幫助，我能很快地適應這裏，並和你們做朋友。

　　我唸大學的時候喜歡在美麗的校園裏和朋友們漫步、談天，我希望以後有時間可以讓我和你們一起重溫那些快樂的回憶。謝謝。

* ***pay a visit to*** 訪問；參觀；遊覽
  at all 全然
  initiative〔 ɪˈnɪʃɪ,etɪv 〕*n.* 進取的精神
  be accustomed to 適應
  be friends with 和～做朋友
  relive〔 riˈlɪv 〕*v.* 再體驗

新生自我介紹(3)

Good morning, teachers and fellow students.
My name is Ching-ming Wang. I am from Taiwan.
I've always been very interested in business, and
have worked very hard at studying it throughout my
four years of college. Unfortunately, the more I
learned, the more I began to realize that I still
don't know enough to do research by myself. I think
I still need a lot more practical experience to make
what I've learned in the classroom more realistic.
So I decided to pursue advanced study at the Harvard School of Business Administration, which I
believe to be the ideal institute for me to get the
experience I need. I hope that I can do a good job
in my pursuits.

This is my first time in America, and also
my first time studying with so many foreign friends.
I hope we will get along very well. My favorite
hobby is shooting pool. I am hoping that I can find
someone here that would like to shoot pool with me.
Thank you.

　　老師、同學們早。我叫王慶銘，來自台灣。我一直對商業很感興趣，在我四年的大學生活中也一直很努力地在研讀。但是不幸地，我學得越多，就越發了解到我所知道的仍然不足以做獨力研究。我想我還需要更多實際的經驗，以使我在課堂上所學到的更爲踏實。因此我決定來哈佛企管研究所深造，我相信這是一所理想的學府，能讓我得到我所需要的經驗，也希望我能做好我的研究工作。

　　這是我第一次來到美國，也是我第一次和這麼多外國朋友一起唸書，希望我們會處得很好。我最喜歡的嗜好是打撞球，我希望能在你們之中找到願意和我打的人。謝謝。

* realistic〔͵riəˈlɪstɪk ͵rɪə-〕*adj.* 實際的
　pursue〔pɚˈsu ͵-ˈsju〕*v.* 追求
　advanced〔ədˈvænst〕*adj.* 高深的
　institute〔ˈɪnstə͵tjut〕*n.* 研究所；大學
　pursuit〔pɚˈsut ͵-ˈsjut〕*n.* 研究工作
　shoot〔ʃut〕*v.* 撞球　　　pool〔pul〕*n.* 撞球戲
　get along(*with~*)（與~）相處；進展

第二章 自我介紹分項歸納

　　在一個聚會中要求參加者做自我介紹的目的，不外是想使大家先有初步的認識，進而增進團體活動的氣氛。所以一篇自我介紹毋須像自傳一般做太多描述，只要做重點介紹，或把自己比較想說的說出來就可以。語氣上儘量保持輕鬆愉快，但是在比較正式的場合，仍須注意用語，例如在輕鬆的場合說："Hi, everybody.",用在會議或帶有考試性質的面談場合中就不適用了。

　　以下參酌第一章的範例，歸納整理出十二個自我介紹可能包含的基本項目與實用例句，並根據各項的內容及各種英文句型，做進一步的分類與評註。讀者看完本章之後再參閱前章的範例，必能完全學會如何用英文對多數人做自我介紹。

1 自我介紹的問侯語

1. (1) Good

morning.	早安。
afternoon.	午安。
evening.	晚安。

(2) Good morning, ladies and gentlemen. 早安，各位先生、女士。

(3) Good morning,

gentlemen.	早安，	各位先生。
ladies.		各位女士。

＊ ladies and gentlemen 是禮貌的問候；(3)用於僅有男士或女士的場合。

(4) Good morning, teachers and fellow students.
老師、同學們早。

(5) Good morning,
| everybody. |
| everyone. |
大家早。

(6)
| Hi, |
| Hello, |
everybody. 嗨，大家好。

  * (5)(6) 適用於較不正式的場合。

2. (1) Good morning. I am very
| glad |
| happy |
| pleased |
to
| be able to |
| have the oppor-tunity |

to
| be here. |
| visit this country. |

早安，我很高興
| 能 |
| 有機會 |
來
| 這裏。 |
| 訪問這個國家。 |

(2) Good morning, ladies and gentlemen. I feel very
| honored |
| privileged |

to
| have the opportunity |
| have been invited |
to
| attend |
| take part in |
| participate in |
this conference.

早安，各位先生，各位女士。我很榮幸
| 有機會 |
| 應邀 |
參加這次會議。

(3) It is a great
| honor |
| privilege |
| pleasure |
for me to be here today, attending

this conference. 今天來這裏參加這次會議是我很大的榮幸。

(4) I feel very honored to attend this conference and shall begin by introducing myself.

我很榮幸參加這次會議，並將先從自我介紹開始。

* (2)(3)(4)適用於正式的場合。

2 介紹姓名

1. My name is Wei-che Ch'en. 我叫陳偉哲。

2. I am David Wang. 我是王大衞。

3 介紹國籍

1. I | am / come | from | Taiwan.
Taiwan, the Republic of China.
the Republic of China, Taiwan.
Free China, Taiwan.

我來自 | 台灣。
台灣，中華民國。
中華民國，台灣。
自由中國，台灣。

2. I am a Chinese, from Taiwan. 我是個來自台灣的中國人。

3. I am Dr. Wu from Taipei, Taiwan. 我是吳博士，來自台北，台灣。

4 介紹自己的職業

1. 工作——

(1) I | am now working for / work for | a | trading company.
publishing house.

我現在在一家 | 貿易公司 / 出版社 | 上班。

(2) ① I work in a | bank.
government institution. |

我在 | 銀行
公家機關 | 做事。

② I teach English in a high school. 我在一所中學教英文。

③ I run a book store. 我經營一家書店。

(3) ① I am a | salesman.
government employee.
housewife. | 我是個 | 推銷員。
公務員。
家庭主婦。 |

② I am a teacher, teaching Chinese in a high school.
我是個老師，在中學教國文。

③ I am a | professor
lecturer | of History | at | Taiwan University.

我是台大的歷史 | 教授。
講師。 |

2. 學生——

(1) ① I am majoring in Chinese at the National Taiwan University. 我在國立台灣大學主修中文。

② I am an economics major at the Chinese Culture University. 我在中國文化大學主修經濟。

③ I am currently a student in the Chinese Department at NTU.
我目前是台大中文系的學生。

④ At present I am studying at Taiwan University, majoring in politics. 我目前就讀於台大，主修政治。

⑤ I am a student at Chengchi University, majoring in social science. 我是政治大學的學生，主修社會科學。

(2) ① I am a graduate student in the history department at Taiwan University. 我是台灣大學歷史系的研究生。

② I am still studying at the National Taiwan Normal University, working on my doctorate.
我還在國立台灣師範大學唸書，攻讀博士學位。

③ I am a third grade student at Jianguo High School.
我是建國中學三年級的學生。

3. 學歷——

(1) 大學畢業

① I graduated from Fu Jen University. 我畢業於輔仁大學。

② I am a graduate of Chung Shan University.
我畢業於中山大學。

③ I graduated from the Department of Business Administration at Chengchi University.
我畢業於政大企管系。

(2) 碩士、博士

① I received a | master's degree / Doctor's degree / Doctoral degree / Doctorate | in Law | at / from | NTU.

我在台大得到法學 | 碩士 / 博士 | 學位。

② I obtained my doctorate from Harvard University.
　我在哈佛大學得到我的博士學位。

③ I have a Doctor of Law from NTU.
　我在台大得到法學博士。

④ I am a | Master | of Foreign languages at NTU.
　　　　　| Doctor |

　　　我是台大外文 | 碩士。 |
　　　　　　　　　| 博士。 |

5 説明來此的原因與目的

1. I was sent by my | company | to attend this conference.
　　　　　　　　　　| country |

　　我被我的 | 公司 | 派來參加這次會議。
　　　　　　 | 國家 |

2. I | should like | to | make more friends, |
　 | want | | learn more useful things, |
　　　　　　　　　　　　| do advanced studies, |
　　　　　　　　　　　　| broaden my horizons, |

　and so I | have come here. |
　　　　　　| am taking part in this conference. |

　我想 | 交更多朋友， |　所以我 | 來到這裏。 |
　　　 | 學更多有用的東西， |　　　 | 參加這次會議。 |
　　　 | 做深入的研究， |
　　　 | 擴展我的視野， |

6 介紹自己的年齡與居住地

1. I am now twenty-two years old, and I live in Taipei.
   我現年22歲,住在台北。

2. I live in Taipei, which is Taiwan's largest city.
   我住在台北,台灣最大的都市。

7 介紹自己的家庭

1. (1) There are six people in my family, including my father, mother, two sisters, one brother and myself.
   我家有六個人,包括我爸爸、我媽媽、兩個姊妹、一個哥哥和我。

   (2) My family consists of my father, mother, a brother and myself. 我家有我爸爸,我媽媽,一個哥哥和我。

   (3) I am the | eldest / youngest | child in my family, and I have

   four brothers and sisters.

   我是家裏最 | 大 / 小 | 的孩子,我有四個兄弟姊妹。

2. (1) I am the only child in my family, but instead of being spoiled, on the contrary, I am very independent.
   我是家裏唯一的小孩,但是我不僅沒有被寵壞,反而很獨立。

   (2) Having been influenced by my family, I love music very much. 由於深受家庭影響,我非常喜愛音樂。

   (3) My father has a bad temper, and perhaps because of genetics, I am apt to get〔become〕angry at times.
   我父親脾氣不好,而也許是遺傳的關係,我有時候很容易生氣。

8 介紹自己的興趣

1. (1) I like | music.
reading and cooking.
sailing for pleasure. |

我喜歡 | 音樂。
看書和烹飪。
划船做消遣。 |

(2) I enjoy | sports, and I like music very much.
getting away from city, and coming into
contact with nature. |

我喜歡 | 運動，並非常喜愛音樂。
離開城市，接觸大自然。 |

(3) I | like
enjoy | many things, | especially
in particular, | music and

reading. 我喜歡很多東西，尤其是音樂和閱讀。

(4) I am interested in | English
biology | very much.

我對 | 英文
生物 | 很感興趣。

2. (1) My | hobby
favorite pastime | is | music.
going to the movies. |

我 | 的嗜好
最喜歡的消遣 | 是 | 音樂。
看電影。 |

⑵ My (favorite)　(greatest)　(usual)　hobbies　interests　pastimes　forms of enjoyment　are reading and

listening to music, | especially classical music. |
| in particular, country music. |

我　（最喜歡的）　（最大的）　（平常的）　嗜好　樂趣　消遣　娛樂　是看書,聽音樂,　尤其是古典音樂。　尤其是鄉村音樂。

⑶ Though I have many interests, photography is what I like most.

我雖然有許多興趣,攝影卻是我最喜歡的。

9 介紹自己的個性

1. 字彙：
outgoing 外向的
extrovert(ed) 外向的
happy-go-lucky 樂天的
cheerful 快活的
curious 好奇的
active 積極的
frank 坦率

introvert(ed) 內向的
reserved 緘默的；內向的
shy 害羞的
bashful 害羞的
timid 膽小的
withdrawn 孤僻的；內向的
passive 被動的；消極的

2. ⑴ I think I am somewhat on the shy side.
我想我有點內向。

(2) I think I am reasonably frank by nature.
我想我生性相當坦率。

(3) I am quite reserved, but I value friendship.
我相當內向，但我重視友誼。

(4) I am a curious person, and I like to learn new things.
我是個好奇的人，喜歡學新的東西。

10 介紹自己的優缺點

1. I am | capable of / good at | playing the piano. / Chinese painting.

我 | 能 / 擅長 | 彈鋼琴。/ 畫國畫。

2. (1) I have a sense of responsibility. 我有責任感。

(2) I approach things very enthusiastically, and I don't like to leave something half-done.
我做事很熱心，而且不喜歡半途而廢。

3. (1) I | am too shy, / tend to be withdrawn, | so I think I | should learn / need

to | open myself up more / become more sociable | and | be more outgoing with people. / spend time with people.

我 | 太害羞， / 容易孤僻， | 所以我想我 | 應該學著 / 必須 | 多開放自己，多和人交往。 / 更喜歡交遊，多和人在一起。

(2) I need to devote more of my time to learning to understand and help others.

我需要花更多時間來學著了解別人，幫助別人。

11 介紹自己的抱負

1. (1) I hope to be a | doctor | one day.
| pianist |

　　　我希望將來做一個 | 醫生。 |
| 鋼琴家。 |

(2) I hope I can bring what I've learned into full play here, and be a good engineer.

　　　我希望我能在這裏發揮所學，並成為一個很好的工程師。

2. My ambition is to become a | diplomat, |
| linguist, |

and | to do some useful things. |
| be fluent in Chinese, Japanese, and English. |

　　　我的抱負是成為一個 | 外交家， | 並 | 做些對國家有用的事。 |
| 語言學家， | | 能說流利的中文、日文 和英文。 |

12 自我介紹的結尾用語

1. **我希望——**

(1) ① I hope everything will go well.

　　　　我希望一切進行順利。

② I hope this 　| conference
seminar |　 will be 　| fruitful.
successful. |

  * seminar〔ˈsɛmə,nɑr,ˌsɛməˈnɑr〕*n.* 研討會

我希望這次 | 會議
研討會 |　| 有豐碩的成果。
成功。 |

(2) ① I hope we will all benefit from this conference.
　　我希望我們都能從此次會議中獲益。

 ② I hope we can increase our mutual co-operation and understanding.
　　我希望我們能增進彼此的合作與了解。

 ③ I hope I can have time to hold discussions with you.
　　我希望我能有時間和你們討論。

 ④ I hope I have the chance to develop my interests and capabilities here.
　　我希望我能有機會在這裏發展我的興趣與能力。

(3) I hope 　| I can become friends with you.
I can become your friend. |

　　我希望 | 我能和你們成爲朋友。
我能成爲你們的朋友。 |

  * (3)適用於對同輩發言，及較不正式的場合。

(4) ① I hope we will 　| have fun
have a good time |　 together.

　　我希望我們能在一起玩得愉快。

② Let's all have a good time. 讓我們大家玩得愉快。

③ I hope everybody has a good time.
我希望每個人都玩得愉快。

④ Let's have fun together. 讓我們一起玩得愉快。

　　* (4)適用於非正式的場合。

2. 結尾——

(1) | In conclusion, | I would like to thank everyone (here)
　　| Finally, |

who | helped make | this gathering | so | enjoyable.
　　| has made | my participation | | meaningful.

最後，我想謝謝（在座）每一位 | 促使 | 這次聚會
　　　　　　　　　　　　　　　| 使 | 我的參與

如此 | 愉快 | 的人。
　　| 富有意義 |

(2) Thank you. 謝謝。

Thank you very much. 非常謝謝。

　　* 禮貌的結尾。

第三章 進一步自我介紹：

談話應注意事項

1 雙向交談

　　想使會話流暢，最重要的是要注意雙方的往來，也就是要有問有答
（ give-and-take ）。因爲單向的往來，會破壞談話的氣氛。試閱下例：

> **A** : Where do you live ?
> 　　你住在那裏？
>
> **B** : Near here.
> 　　附近。
>
> **A** : How near ?
> 　　多近？
>
> **B** : About ten minutes.
> 　　大約十分鐘。
>
> **A** : By bus ?
> 　　搭公車嗎？
>
> **B** : No.
> 　　不是。
>
> **A** : Oh, on foot then ?
> 　　哦，那是走路嗎？
>
> **B** : No.
> 　　不是。

　　從以上的例子可以看出這種會話像是警察在審問犯人似的，非常生
硬。要避免發生這種情況，有簡單的方法可循。

1. 多答幾句———

被問時除了回答對方所問的問題外，要**儘量告訴對方其他相關的事情**，例如：

(1) **A**： Where do you live?

你住在那裏？

B： In a place called Mucha, twenty minutes from here by bus.

我住在一個叫木柵的地方，從這裏搭 20 分鐘的巴士可以到。

(2) **A**： Where do you live?

你住在那裏？

B： For a long time I lived with my wife's parents, but at last we have managed to buy our own house.

很久以來我都跟我岳父岳母住在一起，但是，我們終於設法買了自己的房子。

2. 提出問題———

除上述方法外，可採用乒乓式的會話，也就是在回答了對方問的問題後，再**由自己提出問題問對方**。例如：

A： Where do you live?

你住在那裏？

B： Not far from here, in a company appartment. Does your company provide you with accommodations?

我住在離這裏不遠的員工住宅，你們公司提供住宿嗎？

A : No, I'm afraid not, but I've found a reasonably cheap place to rent. Is your apartment near where you work?

不，恐怕沒有，但是我已經找到租起來相當便宜的地方。你們的住所靠近工作的地方嗎？

B : It's quite a long way away, but the train service is pretty good. Do you travel to work by bus?

相當遠，但是搭火車很方便。你搭公車上班嗎？

以上介紹的兩個技巧非常有效，不僅可以打開談話的僵局，更可以**使談話朝著你所希望的方向發展**。

2 解決特殊情況

1. 在停下來思考時 ——

談話中遇到困難的問題或難以表達的事物時，一般人往往會一時說不出話來。然而如果在思考如何回答時，完全沈默，就難免會被人誤會成你不想回答，而使對方覺得碰了釘子，不想再講下去，因此**回答的表示一定要明確**。關於這點，在這裏介紹幾個技巧：

1. 不要完全沈默，發出 " er〔ɜ〕"（呃…）的聲音，表示正在思考如何回答。

2. 在說出完整的句子前，不妨稍作停頓。也就是先起個頭，這樣對方就會等你說完話。

3. 綜合 1. 2. —— 停頓，並發出語尾音。試閱下例：

(1) A : What would you recommend in this situation?

在這個情況下，你會有什麼建議？

B : I would recommend〔PAUSE...〕that the matter should be reconsidered.

我會建議〔停頓…〕這個案子再作考慮。

(2) **A**： What would you—er—recommend in this—er—
situation ?

在這個——情況下——你會——有什麼建議？

B： I would recommend—er—that we should—er—**refer**
this matter to the—er—administrative section.

我會建議——我們應該——把這個問題交給——管理課。

由此可見，講話停頓不一定會讓人討厭，若表現得宜，反而會予人
慎重而想努力回答的誠懇印象。所以焦急是不必要的，因為事實上不是
每個人對每件事都能作最快的反應，不過在大部分情況下，最好還是儘
快回答，尤其是在輕鬆的場合，**有時不妨隨意地表示一點意見**，或以新
的觀點提出反問，或甚至來一點機智與幽默，例如：

A： What would you do in this situation ?

在這個情況下，你會怎麼做？

B： (a) Well, let me think... yes, what if it **isn't like that**?
for example...

嗯，讓我想想…，對了，如果不一定是那樣呢？**譬如說** …

(b) Well, then you might as well pretend you **don't know**
it. Maybe there will be some other change.

嗯，那倒不如裝作不知道好了，也許另有變化呢！

但是，若真的**一點也想不出時不如坦誠地向對方表示**，並說出你感
到困難的地方，例如：

A： What's your opinion about this ?

關於這點，你有什麼意見？

B： (a) Well, sorry. I'm still not quite sure of the real
situation. I still need to give it some thought.

嗯，**抱歉**，我還不很清楚實際的狀況，我還需要想一想。

(b) Well, could you tell me once again the thing you just mentioned...

　　嗯，你可不可以再跟我說一下你剛剛提到的…

(c) Well, the situation is quite complicated, and I haven't got a clue about it. May I listen to your opinion first?

　　嗯，情況很複雜，我現在還沒有頭緒，可不可以先聽聽你的意見？

　　總結上述各項，讀者多少可以從 B 的回答中，體會出回答者所應有的態度，那就是：誠懇、坦然、與自信，而且也唯有這樣的態度才能使自己無論在任何情況下都能保持鎮定、予人好感，並進而使會話流暢，保有愉快的談話氣氛。

2. 想離席片刻時 ———

　　在談話中偶爾因為要接聽電話、上廁所、或臨時有事而**須離席片刻時，要記住常說 " Excuse me "**，例如：

(1) Excuse me, I must answer the phone.
　　對不起，我得去接電話。

(2) Excuse me, there's somebody at the door.
　　對不起，有人敲門。

(3) Excuse me, I'd just like to... er...
　　對不起，我想去…呃…

　　讀者也許會注意到例(3)並沒有說完，而事實上不須說完，大家也都猜得出這個人是要去上廁所，那麼為什麼不說完呢？這是因為一般人都不喜歡說出 " toilet " 這個字，因此只要大概表示一下就可以了。不過**上廁所還有其他的表示法**，如：

(1) Excuse me, I'd just like to wash my hands.

　　對不起，我只想去洗個手。

(2) Excuse me, I wonder if I could go upstairs for a moment?

　　對不起，我是否可以到樓上去一下？

　　除了用 " Excuse me " 外，**再加上 " Would you " 是更客氣的說法：**

(1) Would you excuse me while I have a word with some other guests？

　　可否請你見諒我和其他客人說幾句話？

(2) Would you be so kind as to excuse me while I say hello to the president？

　　可否請您容我和總裁打個招呼？

　　以上介紹的都是客氣的說法，但是如果氣氛不很嚴肅時，也可以用**比較直接的說法**，如：

(1) Just a moment, there's the phone！ 等一下，有電話。

(2) Hang on, I'll bring another drink.

　　待會兒，我再拿一杯飲料。

(3) I'm just going to wash my hands. I won't be long.

　　我去洗個手，不會去很久。

　　在以上 3 個例句中，例句(3)除了表示有事外，還**表示會繼續回來談話，其他的說法**如下：

(1) I'll be back soon. 我很快就回來。

(2) Please enjoy yourself until I come back.

　　請繼續聊，等我回來。

(3) Don't go away！ 別走開！

談話至中途必須向人告假，可以是小事，也可以是大事。如果能夠熟悉各種說法，自然運用，即時提出，對自己固是絕大的方便，對別人也無所妨礙；反之要是彆在心裏，那麼談話對自己就不啻成了煎熬。所以在這種情況下毋須顧慮太多，只要自然、誠懇地提出即可。

3 小心觸及敏感問題

在剛認識及初交往的階段，最好避免直接問及對方的政治思想、宗教、年齡等，因爲這方面的事，雙方的差別可能很大，而且這很可能是個人較秘密的資料，不是所有人都願意直言相告。因此在觸及這類問題時，**最忌冒然直詢**，如下例：

(1) Who did you vote for in the last election？
上次選舉你投誰的票？

(2) Are you a Christian？ 你是基督徒嗎？

(3) How old are you？ 你幾歲？

這樣的問法很冒昧，會讓人感到突兀，進而**覺得**不舒服。但是這方面的事，固不宜冒然相詢，不過想談時，卻還是**可以用間接的方法**，例如，己方可以表示：

(1) Recently the newspaper mentioned that the clashes between different Islamic factions were very violent. I think that by believing in a religion one can hardly avoid going a little to extremes.
最近報上提到回教各派之間的衝突很激烈，我想信教難免會有點走極端。

(2) If Reagan really has such charisma, then I think he will be the same regardless of the party he belongs to.
如果雷根是這麼得人緣的話，我想他到那一黨都一樣。

(3) I'm not old enough to remember the War.

我沒有那麼大，不記得戰爭的事。

或附帶問對方：

(1) I really like religious music, and you?

我很喜歡宗教音樂，你呢？

(2) I feel that the government's approach this time seems a little inappropriate, don't you agree?

我覺得這次政府的做法好像有點不妥當，你覺得呢？

(3) So did you get married young?

那麼你是早婚了？

　　這樣的說法，顯然比較含蓄，也不致令對方覺得你無禮或有意窺探，而且由於不含明顯而激烈的立場，對方就不致刻意防衛，而能自然地反應回答。這樣不僅談話氣氛能夠保持流暢，你也可以從他的回答，再作進一步的交談，以促進雙方的了解。因此雖然比較費事，但卻是值得的。

　　談話是一種藝術，要求形式與實質的盡美盡善，所以既不應暗藏心機，唇槍舌劍；也不必作機智問答，搶快求勝。一切但求誠懇、自然、輕鬆、與關懷，以俾於人我之間更進一步的交流。

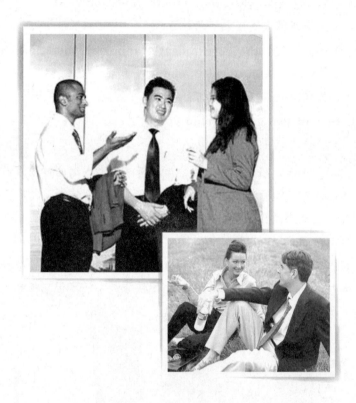

第四章 進一步自我介紹： 實用談話資料

I. 自己・家庭

1. Introducing Myself
自我介紹

1. **A**: Do you mind if I introduce myself？ My name's Chien—
   hsun Ch'en.

   讓我自我介紹好嗎？我叫陳建勳。

   B: How do you do？ My name's Smith—John Smith.

   你好，我叫史密斯——約翰·史密斯。

2. **A**: Hi！ I don't think I've seen you here before. I'm Shu—
   chuan Huang.

   嗨！我想我以前沒在這裏見過你，我是黃淑娟。

   B: Hello！ I'm Jane—Jane Jones.

   嗨！我是珍——珍·瓊斯。

3. **A**: Mr. Green, let me introduce my friend, Wei-ru Ch'en.

   格林先生，讓我介紹我的朋友，陳威如。

   B: I'm very pleased to meet you, Mr. Green.

   很高興和你見面，格林先生。

4. Let me give you my card.

   我給你我的名片。

5. I know a colleague of yours in the finance department.

   我認識你們財政部的一個同事。

6. I'm looking forward to getting to know you better.

   我一直盼望多認識你。

7. Haven't I met you somewhere before ?
　我是不是曾經在那裏見過你 ?

8. I've often heard your name, and was looking forward to meeting you.
　我常常聽到你的名字，並盼望見到你。

9. We have a mutual friend, John White, who may have spoken about me.
　我們都有一個朋友，約翰・懷特，他也許提過我。

10. Do you remember me from last year's conference ? Ching— ming Wang of Continental Bank.
　你記得去年會議的我嗎 ? 大陸銀行的王慶銘。

11. Black — Simon Black — pleased to meet you.
　布萊克——西蒙・布萊克，高興見到你。

12. I'm sorry, could you remind me of your name again, please ?
　抱歉，請你再說一次你的名字好嗎 ?

Note————————————

　1. " 讓我自我介紹 " 可用 Let me introduce myself.

　4. card 名片；卡片　　5. colleague〔'kɑlig〕*n.* 同事
　finance〔fə'næns，'faɪnæns〕*n.* 財政

　6. *look forward to* + *V-ing* 盼望～　　*get to* 變成；著手

　9. mutual〔'mjutʃuəl〕*adj.* 共同的；互相的

　12. *remind sb. of sth.* 使某人想起某事

2. Names
姓 名

1. A : Which of the names on your card is your surname?

你名片上的那個字是你的姓？

B : My family name is Liu. Wei-jung is my given name.

我的姓是劉，偉榮是我的名字。

2. A : What do your initials stand for?

你的姓名字首代表什麼？

B : W is for Wei, and J is for Jung.

W是偉，J是榮。

3. A : Do the characters in your name mean anything?

你名字裏面的字有什麼意思嗎？

B : Oh, yes. The first character is Wei, which means great. Jung, the second one, means glory.

喔，有。第一個字是偉，意思是偉大；榮是第二個字，意思是榮耀。

4. When I was small, I was called Hsiao-hu.

我小時候人家叫我小虎。

5. In Chinese, the family name comes before the given name.

中文的姓在名的前面。

6. Some of the most common surnames in China are Ch'en, Lin, Wang...etc.

中國一些最常見的姓有陳、林、王…等等。

7. Some Chinese people have compound surnames, which come from the combination of two characters, such as Si Ma, Ou Yang, Nan Gong etc. 有些中國人有複姓，也就是由兩個字組成的姓，例如：司馬、歐陽、南宮等等。

8. Some Chinese siblings share a common character in their names, for example：Shu-hua, Shu-ling, Shu-fen, etc. 有些中國人的兄弟或姊妹的名字共用一個字，例如淑華、淑玲、淑芬等等。

9. It is sometimes possible to tell a Western family's original profession from their last name, for instance Silversmith, Shoemaker, etc. 有時候可以從西方人的姓說出他們家族原來的職業，例如西爾弗史密斯、修馬克等等。

10. Many Western names are passed down through the family for generations, hence there may be a Roderick T., Jones the seventh. 很多西方人的名字是家族世代傳下來的，因此也許會有羅德瑞克T，約翰七世等名字。

11. Japanese add -*san* to somebody's name when they talk to them or about them. 日本人在對某人講話或提到某人時，把-*san*加在他名字的後面。

12. Japanese girls' names often end in -*ko*. 日本女孩的名字最後常有個-*ko*。

Note ――――――――

1. surname 姓，= family〔last〕name　　given name 名，=personal〔first〕name

2. initial〔ɪ'nɪʃəl〕*n.* （姓名的）第一個字母；字首　　***stand for*** 代表；象徵

3. character 字母；特質

8. sibling〔'sɪblɪŋ〕*n.* 兄(弟)；姊(妹)　　9. smith 鐵匠　　shoemaker 鞋匠

3.Age and Date of Birth
年齡・出生年月日

1. **A**: What is your date of birth, please?
   請問你的生日是什麼時候?

   B: May 10, 1948.
   1948年5月10日。

2. **A**: What year of the Republic were you born in?
   你是民國幾年生的?

   B: 37 — that's 1948 by the Western calendar.
   37年——也就是西元 1948年。

3. **A**: Would you mind telling me your age?
   你介意告訴我你的年齡嗎?

   B: Well, I'll be 36 later this year; right now I'm still 35.
   嗯,今年年尾我就滿36歲,現在還是35歲。

4. I'd rather not tell you how old I am.
   我寧願不告訴你我幾歲。

5. I had my 20th birthday just a few days ago.
   就在幾天前,我過了20歲的生日。

6. What a coincidence! My birthday's May 10, too!
   好巧!我的生日也是 5 月 10 日。

7. I was born three years after the end of the War.
   我是戰後三年出生的。

8. Some people often do not say how old they are or ask how old you are, but say which year they were born or ask which year you were born instead. 有些人常常不說「我幾歲」，或問「你幾歲？」，而說「我是幾年次」，「你是幾年次？」。

9. I was born in the year of the rat.
   我是鼠年生的。

10. There is a cycle of twelve years, each with a different animal.
   有十二年的週期，每年都有一隻不同的動物（十二生肖）。

11. My boss was born in the year of the rat before me, which means that he's 12 years older.
   我的老闆在我前一個鼠年出生，那表示他比我大 12 歲。

12. If you don't want to reveal your age, give the name of an animal not in the cycle, like cat or elephant.
   如果你不想透露你的年齡，就說一個不在週期（十二生肖）裏的動物，如貓或象。

Note ───────

3. Would you mind + *V-ing* ? 你介意～嗎？

4. *Would rather* 寧願

6. coincidence〔koˈɪnsədəns〕*n.* 巧合；一致

4. Place of Birth/Hometown
出生地・故鄉

1. **A**: What part of the country do you come from?
   你是那裏人？

   B: I am from Hsin-hua in Tainan.
   我是台南新化人。

2. **A**: What sort of place is it?
   那是什麼樣的地方？

   B: It's a town about 300 kilometers south of Taipei.
   那是在台北以南約300公里的一個鎮。

3. **A**: Do you go back there very often?
   你常常回去嗎？

   B: Usually I take my family back twice a year, at
   Lunar New Year and for the Tomb Sweeping Festival.
   我通常一年帶我的家人回去兩次，在舊曆年和清明節時。

4. I only lived there until I was about 11, but I still
   regard it as my hometown.
   我只有在那裏住到大約11歲，但是我仍然把它當作我的故鄉。

5. Up to my grandfather's generation my family were the
   local soy-sauce manufacturers.
   從我祖父那一代起，我家就是本地的醬油製造商。

6. I enjoy sitting with my relatives, eating the local food and talking about old times.

   我喜歡和我的親戚坐著吃本地的東西，談談以前的時代。

7. When I retire, I'd like to move back and take it easy for the rest of my life. 等我退休時,我想搬回去悠閒地過下半輩子。

8. My wife comes from a fishing port called Nan-fang-ao, on the coast of the Pacific.

   我太太來自一個叫南方澳的漁港，這漁港臨太平洋。

9. There's a magnificent view of a few islands, and the fish there is delicious.

   那裏有幾個小島，風景很美，那裏的魚也很好吃。

10. Last fall my father passed away so my wife and I went back to our hometown for the funeral.

   去年秋天，我父親去世，我和我太太回故鄉去奔喪。

Note ────────────

hometown 故鄉

1. A = Where do you come from ?　　3. Lunar New Year 農曆新年

4. *regard ～ as* … 把～視爲…　　5. soy sauce 醬油

7. *take it easy* 悠然自得

9. delicious〔dɪ'lɪʃəs〕*adj.* 美味的　　10. *pass away* 去世

funeral〔'fjunərəl〕*n.* 葬禮

5. When I Was Small
小 時 候

1. **A**： Where did you grow up？
   你在那裏長大？

   B： When I was small I lived in a little village in the middle of the countryside.
   我小時候住在鄉下的小村裏。

2. **A**： What do you remember best？
   你記得最清楚的是什麼？

   B： I remember running round catching insects, fishing and climbing trees.
   我記得跑來跑去地抓蟲、釣魚、和爬樹。

3. **A**： How did you get on at school？
   你在學校唸得怎樣？

   B： At elementary school I did better than average, even though I don't remember studying very much.
   小學我唸得比一般人好，雖然我不記得我很用功。

4. I used to get really sunburnt from playing outside all day.
   我以前曾因為整天在外面玩，而曬得很黑。

5. When I was in the second grade I caught chicken pox and measles and had to spend a long time in bed.
   我二年級的時候得了水痘和麻疹，得在床上躺很久。

6. I'm afraid I was a bit of a bully, which caused my parents a lot of trouble.

恐怕我有點愛欺負人，那替我爸媽惹來了很多麻煩。

7. My parents made me take piano lessons, but I gave up after a short time. 我父母讓我學鋼琴，但是我沒多久就放棄了。

8. I was crazy about the stars, and pestered my father into buying me a telescope.

我對星星著了迷，吵著要我爸爸買一架望遠鏡。

9. I could eat almost anything. The only thing I didn't really enjoy was bitter-melon.

我幾乎什麼都能吃，我唯一不喜歡的東西就是苦瓜。

10. My greatest passion was reading, and I preferred that to going out to play.

我最大的嗜好是看書，我喜歡看書甚於出去玩。

11. When I was a child, I had many friends I played with, but since we have grown up, we have not made contact any-more. 我小時候有許多玩伴，只是長大以後就沒有再聯絡。

Note ————————————

1. countryside *n.* 鄉間；鄉村地方
4. sunburnt *adj.* 曬黑的（為 sunburn 的過去分詞，= sunburned）
5. pox〔pɑks〕*n.* 水痘（= chicken pox）　measles〔'mizlz〕*n.* 麻疹
6. *a bit of a* (*n*) ～ 有點～　bully〔'bʊlɪ〕*n.* 欺凌弱小者
8. *be crazy about* 對～著迷　pester〔'pɛstɚ〕*v.* 煩擾
9. bitter-melon 苦瓜　10. passion〔'pæʃən〕*n.* 熱情；愛好
prefer ～ to … 喜歡～甚於…

6. At University (1)
大 學 (1)

1. **A :** What school did you graduate from ?

   你是什麼學校畢業 ?

   B : I graduated from Chung Shan University, which is located in Kaohsiung's Hsi-tzu Wan.

   我畢業於中山大學,學校在高雄的西子灣。

2. **A :** When were you in college ?

   你什麼時候唸大學 ?

   B : I started in 1966, and graduated in 1970.

   我 1966年入學,畢業於 1970 年。

3. **A :** Was it difficult to get in ?

   要進去很難嗎 ?

   B : There were six candidates for every place, but I was lucky.

   每六個應考的人才錄取一個,但是我很幸運。

4. I failed at my first attempt and had to study for one more year before taking the exams again.

   我第一次嚐試失敗,必須多唸一年再參加考試。

5. I got into my second choice, but in the end I didn't accept the place I was offered.

   我上了第二志願,但後來沒有去唸。

6. Studying at the Normal University is not only tuition-free, but there's also a monthly stipend. However, one must serve an internship for one year after graduation.

唸師範大學不僅免費，每月還有補助，只是畢業後要實習一年。

7. I lived at home and travelled in by train and bus every day.

我住在家裏，每天坐火車和公車上學。

8. My tutor held a seminar once a week.

我的教授每週開一次研討會。

9. Our text was Keynes' *General Theory*, and we were made to work pretty hard.

我們的課題是凱因斯的總體理論，我們被逼得很用功。

10. The library had a good selection of English and French literature, but I hardly used it.

圖書館有很好的英法文選，但我很少用。

Note ————————

3. candidate〔ˈkændə,det , ˈkændədɪt〕*n.* 應考（以求學或求職）者

6. stipend〔ˈstaɪpɛnd〕*n.* 補助金　　internship〔ˈɪntɜn,ʃɪp〕*n.* 實習

8. tutor〔ˈtutɚ, ˈtjutɚ〕*n.*〔英大學〕個別指導教授

seminar〔ˈsɛmə,nɑr , ,sɛməˈnɑr〕*n.* 研討會

7. At University (2)
大 學 (2)

1. **A**: What did you major in?
   你主修什麼?

   B: My major was engineering.
   我主修工程。

2. **A**: Do you attend a public or private university?
   你唸公立大學還是私立大學?

   B: I attend a private university and the expenses are 3 or 4 times more than at a public university.
   我唸私立大學,學費比公立貴了三、四倍。

3. **A**: How many classes did you have during the week?
   你一個禮拜得上多少課?

   B: I don't remember exactly how many, but with lectures, seminars and experiments there seemed to be no time for anything else. 上多少課我記不清楚,但是講課、研討課、加上實驗三種,似乎就沒有時間做別的事了。

4. I lived in lodgings within walking distance of the campus.
   我租房子住,走路可以到學校。

5. My tutor was a well-known expert in the field of control engineering and had published several books on the subject.
   我的教授是很有名的控制工程專家,並且在這方面出了幾本書。

6. I took a part-time job teaching math to young children to support myself.
   我兼差教小孩數學來供給我自己 。

7. Unlike many other countries, the academic year begins in April. 跟其他許多學校不同的是 ，學年從四月開始 。

8. There are two terms, with two long vacations between them. 有2學期中間有兩個長的假期 。

9. During the long summer vacations I should have studied but instead I spent most of the time enjoying myself, or working to get money.
   在漫長的暑假中我應該用功 ，但是我反而花了大部分時間來玩 ，或工作賺錢 。

10. Our school library has the largest collection of book stocks in the country.
    我們學校的圖書館是全國藏書最多的 。

Note ────────────

1. major 〔美〕主修 ，=〔英〕specialize　　3. lecture 〔ˈlɛktʃɚ〕*n.* 講課
4. lodging 〔ˈlɑdʒɪŋ〕*n.*〔*pl.*〕出租宿舍　campus 〔ˈkæmpəs〕*n.*〔美〕校園
9. *enjoy oneself* 享樂　10. stock 〔stɑk〕*n.* 儲藏

8. Campus Life
學生生活

1. **A**: Were you very active in college?
   你在大學很活躍嗎？

   B: I joined a tennis club and the Organization of Student Representatives. 我參加網球社和代聯會。

2. **A**: How did you spend your time outside classes?
   你課餘時間做什麼事？

   B: I'm afraid I wasted a lot of time playing table tennis, or just drinking coffee and talking.
   我恐怕花了很多時間打乒乓球，或只是喝咖啡、談天。

3. **A**: What's your happiest memory of university life?
   在你大學生活中最快樂的回憶是什麼？

   B: Making a lot of good friends and being able to do what I liked in my free time.
   交很多好朋友，能夠在我空閒的時候做我喜歡做的事。

4. My university had one campus **downtown**, and a new one out in the suburbs.
   我的學校在市中心有一個校區，新校區在郊外。

5. There were 26 sports clubs, and over 30 for cultural activities. 有26個體育社團，30多個文化性社團。

6. I represented my university at several English speech contests. 我代表我的學校參加了幾次英文演講比賽。

7. I was a member of the Chinese boxing club, but I wasn't very enthusiastic about taking part in its activities.
我是國術社的一員，但是我不很熱衷於參加活動。

8. I was on the committee of the folk-song society, in charge of recruiting new members.
我是民謠會的委員，負責招收新會員。

9. Every year we plan an open house on our school's birthday and invite students from other schools to attend.
我們每年都舉辦園遊會，邀請其他學校的學生來玩。

10. Frequently there are lectures at school in the evening, so it is more convenient for those who live in the dorms to attend. 學校在晚上常常有演講，所以住宿舍的人比較方便去聽。

11. Of course the first purpose of a university is study, but the social life is also very important for character development.
當然大學的首要目標是求學，但是社會生活對人格的成長也很重要。

12. The administrative experience I gained through participating in student organizations gives me more confidence in dealing with people.
我在社團得到的行政經驗，使我在待人處世方面倍增信心。

Note ————————

8. society 會；社會 *in charge of* 負責（照料）
recruit〔rɪ'krut〕*v.* 招收（新兵或新成員）
10. dorm〔dɔrm〕*n.*〔口〕宿舍（= domitory）

9. Study Abroad
留 學

1. **A**: So you studied abroad?
   所以你去留學？

   B: I got an M.A. in economics at the University of Southern California in the United States.
   我在美國的南加大得到經濟學碩士。

2. **A**: How did you enjoy studying in the States?
   你在美國唸得怎樣？

   B: It was difficult to keep up with all the reading and essay assignments.
   很難跟上全部的讀書和論文作業。

3. **A**: What part did you find the most useful?
   你覺得那些最有用？

   B: I picked up a lot of knowhow from case-studies of business administration.
   我從企業管理的個案研究中得到了很多實用知識。

4. My American room-mate was really kind to me.
   我的美國室友對我眞好。

5. I still keep in touch with the family I stayed with.
   我仍然和我住過的家庭保持聯絡。

6. As I made a point of going around with English speakers as much as possible, I think my English improved a lot.
   因爲我注意儘可能和說英文的人在一起，我想我的英文進步很多。

7. Another Chinese I knew spent all of his time with other Chinese students, and his English made no progress.
   我認識的另一個中國人大部分時候都跟其他的中國學生在一起，他的英文就沒有進步。

8. I had an American girlfriend, and we used to go out driving or dancing on weekends.
   我有一個美國女朋友，我們習慣在週末開車或跳舞。

9. I thought I might have a hard time getting back into Taiwanese society. 我想我回到台灣的社會也許會有一段困難的時期。

10. Some people get too Americanized and don't seem to fit in Chinese companies.
    有些人變得太美國化，似乎和中國的朋友格格不入。

Note ————————————

3. ***pick up*** 得到；拾起
   know-how *n*. 實用知識；要訣
5. ***keep in touch with*** 和～保持聯絡
6. ***make a point of*** (＋*V-ing*) 重視；堅持
10. ***fit in*** (*with* ～) (和～) 相合

10. Where I Live
住的地方

1. **A**: Tell me about where you live.
   告訴我你住在那裏。

   B: I live in the suburbs of Taipei, which is Taiwan's largest city.
   我住在台北近郊，台北是台灣最大的都市。

2. **A**: How long does it take you to get to work?
   你去上班要多久的時間？

   B: Ten minutes by bus to the station, and then 40 minutes on the train into Taipei.
   搭十分鐘的巴士到車站，再坐四十分鐘火車到台北。

3. **A**: Are there any fun places where you live?
   你家那邊有什麼好玩的地方？

   B: There's a circle near my house where there are a lot of places to eat and the night market is very lively.
   我家那邊有個圓環，那裏有很多小吃店，晚上的夜市很熱鬧。

4. I live near the center of Taoyuan.
   我住在靠近桃園市中心的地方。

5. There's a railroad crossing near my house so it is quite noisy sometimes.
   我家附近有平交道通過，所以有時候蠻吵的。

6. The city I live in is the prefecture's administrative center.

　我住的城市是那個縣的行政中心。

7. I live in a newly established residential area and the transportation is very convenient.

　我住在新建的住宅區，交通很方便。

8. Just ten minutes' walk from my house there's an old temple, and its grounds are now used as a park.

　從我家只要走十分鐘就有一間古廟，它的地現在已用作公園。

9. My house is on a hill facing the sea, and so it's cool in summer and warm in winter.

　我家在面海的山丘上，所以夏涼多暖。

10. There's a small stream near my house with willows on the banks. It's beautiful scenery.

　我家附近有一條小溪，溪邊有柳樹，風景很優美。

Note

1. the suburbs （都市的）近郊　　3. circle〔'sɝkḷ〕*n*. 圓環
night market 夜市　　　　　　lively 熱鬧的；有生氣的
5. railroad crossing 平交道　　6. prefecture〔'prifɛktʃɚ〕*n*. 縣
7. residential〔,rɛzə'dɛnʃəl〕*adj*. 住宅的

11. My House
房　子

1. **A**： How big is your house ?

   你家有多大？

   B： It has five rooms— two upstairs and three downstairs.

   我家有五個房間—— 二間在樓上，三間在樓下。

2. **A**： Do you live in a bungalow or a storeyed house ?

   你家是平房還是樓房？

   B： A bungalow. In fact it's a wooden Japanese-style house which are very rare in Taipei these days.

   平房，而且是木造的日本式房子，這在台北已經很少見了。

3. **A**： Your house must have been pretty expensive.

   你的房子一定相當貴。

   B： That's the most expensive housing in Taipei.

   那裏就是台北市最貴的房子。

4. My home hardly has room to swing a cat, but it would cost nearly 3 million NT.

   我家幾乎連讓貓轉身的空間都沒有，但是卻幾乎要台幣3百萬元。

5. I could never borrow that much on my salary ; I inherited the house from my father.

   我從薪水怎樣也弄不到那麼多錢；我是從我父親那裡繼承了這棟房子。

6. My two children have a room each, my wife and I share a room, and then we have a living room and a dining room.

我的兩個小孩每人有一個房間，我妻子和我共用一間，然後有一間客廳和餐廳。

7. We have central heating and air conditioning, which makes the house quite comfortable.

我們有中央暖氣和空調設備，使房子住起來相當舒服。

8. It's in a pleasant area, not far from shops and schools.

那是個舒適的地方，離商店和學校不遠。

9. We live in a seven- story apartment which has 30 pings— a ping is the same as 35 sq. ft. 我們住在一棟七層的公寓裏，有三十多坪——一坪等於 35 平方英尺。

10. You're welcome to come have a look if you have time. It's completely European style including the architecture and interior decoration.

你有空可以來看，那是純歐洲式的，包括外觀和內部裝潢。

Note ————————————

2. bungalow〔'bʌngə,lo〕*n.* 平房 storeyed〔'stɔrɪd〕*adj.* 樓的

4. *no room to swing a cat* (*in*) 連使貓轉身的空間都沒有（地方太狹窄）

9. square〔skwɛr〕*n.* 平方

10. architecture〔'ɑrkə,tɛktʃɚ〕*n.* 建築的設計或式樣

12.My Wife/My Husband
太太・先生

1. **A**: How did you meet your wife ?
   你怎麼遇見你太太？

   B: We met at a tennis club we used to go to.
   我們在我們常去的一個網球俱樂部遇到的。

2. **A**: What kind of wedding did you have ?
   你們的婚禮採用什麼方式？

   B: We had a court wedding first and then held a ban-
   quet in a restaurant.
   我們先公證結婚，然後在餐館請客。
   We had a religious ceremony in the church.
   我們在教堂舉行宗教婚禮。

3. **A**: Have you been married long ?
   你們結婚很久了嗎？

   B: It doesn't seem so long, but we had our tenth wedding anniversary last month.
   好像沒那麼久，但是上個月我們過了十週年結婚紀念日。

4. **O**urs was an arranged marriage. 我們是媒妁婚姻。

5. **W**e were introduced by the professor who tutored me
   in college.
   我們是由在大學指導我的教授介紹的。

6. My wife used to work in a kindergarten.
   我太太以前在幼稚園工作。

7. My husband is a few years older than me.
   我丈夫比我大幾歲。

8. We have our ups and downs, but generally speaking we
   are happily married.
   我們有我們的起伏，但是大體上來說，我們有美滿的婚姻。

9. I usually call my wife by her nickname.
   我通常叫我太太的小名。

10. My husband is handy with jobs about the house.
    我先生很會做家裏的活。

11. I don't help my wife with the housework as much as I
    should. 我沒盡我應盡之力來幫太太做家事。

12. This is my wife, Mei-fen.
    這是我太太，美芬。

Note ————————————

2. wedding〔'wɛdɪŋ〕*n.* 婚禮　　court～ 公證結婚
3. anniversary〔,ænə'vɝsərɪ〕*n.* 週年紀念（日）
4. arranged marriage 媒妁婚姻
5. tutor〔'tutɚ, 'tjutɚ〕*v.* （個別）指導；家教
8. ***ups and downs*** 起伏　　9. nickname〔'nɪk,nem〕*n.* 綽號；小名
10. handy〔'hændɪ〕*adj.* 熟練的

13.Children
孩　子

1. **A**：How many children do you have？
   你們有幾個小孩？

   B：We have two — a boy and a girl.
   我們有兩個小孩—— 一男一女。

2. **A**：Which one is the elder？
   那個比較大？

   B：Our daughter. There is a saying in Chinese that it's good to have a daughter first, then a son.
   女兒。中國人說先有女兒再有兒子很好。

3. **A**：Have you got a photograph of your family？
   你有你家的照片嗎？

   B：Yes, here you are. That's my son on the right. His name's Ch'en-chung.
   有，在這裏。在右邊的是我兒子，他叫辰中。

4. Two children is the ideal number as promoted by family planning in Taiwan.
   兩個小孩是台灣推行家庭計畫的理想數目。

5. Sometimes we think it would be nice to have one more child.
   有時候我們想再多一個孩子一定很好。

6. They are both quite a handful. 他們兩個都很難管。

7. Mei‐fang my daughter, is getting on very well at school.
我女兒美芳，在學校唸得很好。

8. Ch'en‐chung goes to a supplementary school once a week to prepare for the extrance exams.
辰中每個禮拜上一次補習班，準備入學考試。

9. He's addicted to video games, which makes his mother angry at times.
他沈迷於電視遊樂器，有時會讓他媽媽生氣。

10. They hardly see their father during the week.
他們一星期難得看到他們的爸爸。

11. On weekends I play with them or take them out.
週末我和他們玩，或帶他們出去。

12. She used to say she wanted to be a nurse, but now she wants to be a pop star.
她以前說她想當護士，但是現在想當歌星。

Note ──────────

2. saying 諺語；格言

6. handful〔'hænd, fʊl, 'hæn‐〕*n.*〔口〕難控制的人；棘手的事

8. supplementary school 補習班　　9. *be addicted to* 沈迷

at times 有時　　12. pop〔pɑp〕*adj.* 流行的　　*n.* 流行歌曲

14. Parents
父 母 親

1. **A：** Tell me about your parents.
   跟我說說你的父母。

   B： My father died six years ago.
   我父親在六年前去世。

2. **A：** I'm sorry to hear that. Is your mother in good health？
   聽你這麼說我很難過。你母親身體好吧？

   B： Yes, thank you. She's very active for her age.
   是的，謝謝你。以她的年齡來說，她非常活躍。

3. **A：** What's your father's job？
   你父親做什麼事？

   B： He worked for a bank until he was 60, and then he retired.
   他在一家銀行做到60歲，然後退休。

4. My mother gets a pension from where my father used to work.
   我母親從我父親以前工作的地方領到退休金。

5. I'm afraid my mother tends to spoil her grandchildren.
   我怕我母親會寵壞她的孫子。

6. My father suffers from asthma in the winter.
   我父親在冬天會發氣喘病。

7. After my father retired, my parents moved to a small house near the sea.
我父親退休以後，父母就搬到一間靠海的房子。

8. They like us to take the children to visit them occasionally. 他們喜歡我們偶爾帶小孩去看他們。

9. Their latest hobby is traveling, and they've been almost everywhere in Taiwan.
他們近來喜歡旅行，而且幾乎已經到過台灣每個地方。

10. My father seems to have too much spare time since he retired. 我父親自從退休以後，似乎太空閒了。

11. I don't know what I would have done without my parents' support when I was younger.
我不知道年輕的時候，如果沒有父母親的支持會怎樣。

Note ——————

4. pension〔'pɛnʃən〕 *n.* 退休金；養老金   5. *tend to* 易於

6. asthma〔'æsmə, 'æzmə〕*n.* 哮喘   10. spare time 餘暇

15. Brothers & Sisters
兄弟姐妹

1. **A**: Do you have any brothers and sisters?
   你有兄弟姊妹嗎?

   B: Yes, I have two brothers and a sister.
   有,我有兩個兄弟和一個妹妹。

2. **A**: Are you the eldest?
   你是最大的嗎?

   B: No, I'm the second child. I have one brother older than me.
   不,我是老二,我有一個兄弟比我大。

3. **A**: What do your brothers and sisters do?
   你的兄弟姊妹做什麼事?

   B: My elder brother's a journalist, my younger brother is training to be an architect, and my sister's still in college.
   我哥哥是記者,我弟弟正在受訓當建築師,我妹妹還在上大學。

4. I haven't seen my elder brother for a couple of years.
   我已經幾年沒看到我哥哥了。

5. My sister got married to a lawyer last month.
   我姊姊上個月嫁給一個律師。

6. My brother has just got engaged.
   我哥哥剛訂婚。

7. I'm an only child.
   我是唯一的小孩。

8. Can you see any family resemblance in my sister and me?
   你可以看出我和我妹妹有家人之間相像的地方嗎？

9. You can tell my twin brother and me apart by this mark
   on my cheek.
   你可以從我臉上的疤痕分辨出我和我的孿生兄弟。

10. My sister and I are 12 years apart.
    我妹妹和我差 12 歲。

11. There's only a year between my brothers.
    我們兄弟之間只差一歲。

Note ─────────

4. *a couple of* 幾個；兩個　　6. engaged〔ɪn'gedʒd〕*adj.* 已訂婚的
8. resemblance〔rɪ'zɛmbləns〕*n.* 相似（之處）
family～ 血親間的類似
9. *tell～apart* 分辨～　　mark *n.* 記號；疤痕

16. Physical Features
身體的特徵

1. **A**: How tall are you ?
   你有多高？

   B: I'm 1 m 72 cm tall, which is above the Chinese average.
   我高 1 公尺 72 公分，比中國人的平均高。

2. **A**: How much do you weigh ?
   你有多重？

   B: The last time I weighed myself I weighed 65kg,
   which is about average for my height.
   我上次量我自己是 65 公斤，就我的身高而言，差不多合標準。

3. **A**: Are you near-sighted or far-sighted ?
   你是近視還是遠視？

   B: I'm near-sighted in my right eye.
   我右眼近視。

4. I've been wearing glasses since I was in college.
   我從上大學開始，就一直戴眼鏡。

5. In English, you would say my eyes are brown, but in
   Chinese they're black. 用英文，你會說我的眼睛是棕色的，
   但用中文來說是黑色的。

6. My hair used to be black, but now it's going gray in
   places. 我頭髮以前是黑的，但現在很多地方都變灰了。

7. I've lost a bit of hair at the front since I turned 40.
   我過了四十歲以後，前額就掉了一些頭髮。

8. I got this scar in an accident on my bicycle when I was 16.
   我 16 歲騎脚踏車，在一次意外中留下了這個疤。

9. I used to be slimmer, but now I've put on some weight around the middle.
   我以前比較瘦，不過現在腰部已經胖了一些。

10. If I could lose a little weight, I'd have a much sportier figure.
    如果我能減少一些體重，我就很有運動員的身材了。

11. I've always been on the small side.
    我一直是小號。

12. There's nothing I can do about my bad posture.
    我對我的姿態不佳毫無辦法。

13. I got this suntan playing golf the other day.
    前幾天我打高爾夫球晒黑了。

Note ——————————————

6. *in places* 多處；到處　　7. front 前面；額
turn 超過（某年齡、時間、金額）　　8. scar 疤
9. slim 瘦細的　　*put on* 增加；穿上
the middle 腰部；中央　　10. sport 運動的
11. *on the small side* 顏小；在小的一邊　　12. posture〔'pɑstʃɚ〕*n.* 姿勢
13. suntan〔'sʌntæn〕*n.* (皮膚)曬黑　　the other day 前幾天

17. Health
健　康

1. **A**： How is your health ?
   你的健康如何？

   B： Fortunately very good ; I've never had a day's illness in my life.
   很幸運非常好，我這輩子從來沒有生過一天病。

2. **A**： How often do you get a check-up ?
   你多久做一次健康檢查？

   B： I make a point of having a check-up twice a year.
   我每年一定做兩次健康檢查。

3. **A**： How do you keep your weight down ?
   你怎樣保持你的體重？

   B： Every morning, rain or shine, I jog for 30 minutes.
   每天早上，不論晴雨，我都慢跑 30 分鐘。

4. Recently my teeth have needed attention and I've been going to the dentist pretty frequently.
   最近我的牙齒需要注意，我就常常去看牙醫。

5. At my age I have to watch my blood pressure.
   在我這個年紀，我得注意血壓。

6. I have myself screened for cancer whenever I can ; early detection is important in curing it.
   我儘可能預防癌症；早期發現對治療很重要。

7. When I was a child I had an operation for appendicitis.

我小時候動過盲腸炎手術。

8. I fell down the stairs at home and broke my arm.

我在家裏的樓梯上跌倒，弄斷了手臂。

9. My wife has not been in very good shape, and she has taken up tennis to get fit.

我太太近來身體不大好，她就開始打網球來增進健康。

10. My son spent a week in bed with a bad cold.

我兒子得重感冒，在床上躺了一星期。

11. I have health insurance, and so I don't need to worry about medical costs.

我有健康保險，所以不必擔心醫藥費。

12. My grandfather is a firm believer in Chinese medicine because his illness was cured with Chinese medicine.

我祖父非常信中藥，因爲他的病就是吃中藥好的。

Note ——————————————

2. check-up *n.* 健康檢查　***make a point of*** 必定

3. ***keep down*** 使不增加；控制　***rain or shine*** 不論晴雨　jog〔dʒɑg〕*v.* 慢跑

5. blood pressure 血壓　6. screen 遮蔽　detection 發覺

7. appendicitis〔ə,pɛndə'saɪtɪs〕*n.* 盲腸炎　9. ***in good shape*** 情況好

take up 開始　　fit 健康的　　10. a bad cold 重感冒

12. Chinese medicine 中藥

18. Food & Meals
餐　食

1. **A**： How many meals a day do you have？
   你一天吃幾餐？

   B： I eat three meals a day；the biggest is my evening meal．
   我一天吃三餐；最主要的是晚餐。

2. **A**： What do you have for breakfast？
   你早餐吃什麼？

   B： I usually only have time for a cup of coffee and a piece of toast．
   我通常只有時間喝一杯咖啡和吃一片烤麵包。

3. **A**： Do you usually eat at home？
   你通常在家裏吃嗎？

   B： Yes，I eat at home as much as I can．I only go to restaurants when I go out with friends．
   是的，我儘量在家裏吃，和朋友出去才上館子。

4. In the evening I have a reasonably typical Chinese meal of fish or meat, vegetables, a bowl of soup and a bowl of rice.
   晚上我吃相當典型的中餐，有魚或肉、蔬菜、一碗湯和一碗飯。

5. If I go to bed later than usual I usually have a midnight snack which consists of just a bowl of congee and a salted duck egg.
   我晚睡的時候通常會吃宵夜，只要一碗稀飯和一個鹹鴨蛋就可以了。

6. Keeping frozen boiled pork dumplings in the refrigerator is very convenient because you can cook them up to eat at any time.

把冷凍水餃冰在冰箱，可以隨時煮來吃，非常方便。

7. I enjoy cooking myself, and I'm not bad at making Chinese food.

我喜歡自己做菜，我中國菜做得不錯。

8. I'm lucky that my wife is such a good cook.

我很幸運，我太太是個很好的廚師。

9. Some people say Chinese food is too greasy.

有人說中國菜太油。

10. In some countries, certain kinds of meat are forbidden, but there is nothing like that in China.

在有些國家，吃某些肉是禁止的，但是中國沒有這樣的事。

Note ─────────

1. meal （一日間定時的）餐　　2. toast 烤麵包；土司

5. midnight snack 宵夜　congee〔'kɑndʒi〕*n.* 稀飯

6. dumpling〔'dʌmplɪŋ〕*n.* 蒸或煮的麵團

boiled pork dumplings 水餃

9. greasy〔'grisɪ, 'grizɪ〕*adj.* 多油脂的

19.Favorite Foods
喜歡吃的東西

1. **A**: What is your favorite food ?
   你最喜歡吃什麼東西？

   B: What I like best is lobster, but it's too expensive for me to eat very often.
   我最喜歡吃龍蝦，但是它太貴了，我不能常常吃。

2. **A**: Is there anything you don't like ?
   有什麼你不喜歡吃的嗎？

   B: Ever since I was a child I haven't liked onions very much.
   我從小就不大喜歡吃洋蔥。

3. **A**: What do you feel like eating right now ?
   你現在喜歡吃什麼？

   B: If I had a choice, I'd like to get my teeth into a nice, thick steak.
   如果我可以選的話，我想啃一塊又好又厚的牛排。

4. I could never get tired of eating eggs.
   蛋我從來吃不厭。

5. I enjoy any fruit that's in season.
   我喜歡吃任何應時的水果。

6. Unless I cut down on the number of chocolate cakes I eat, I'll get very fat.
   除非我少吃巧克力蛋糕，否則會變很胖。

7. One thing I like about summer is eating cold noodles dipped in a special sauce.

　　我喜歡夏天的一點就是吃特別浸在調味汁裏的涼麵。

8. I like Western meal very much.

　　我很喜歡吃西餐。

9. When I was a child, I didn't like spinach, but I don't mind it now.

　　我小時候不喜歡吃菠菜，但現在不覺得了。

10. My children don't like carrots, but I make them eat them.

　　我的小孩不喜歡吃紅蘿蔔，但我強迫他們吃。

11. I must admit that I only eat cabbage because I know it's good for me.

　　我得承認我只吃甘藍菜，因爲我知道那對我有益。

12. Westerners don't eat animal entrails, but Chinese eat them with relish.

　　西方人不吃動物的內臟，但中國人卻吃得津津有味。

Note ————————

1. lobster〔'lɑbstɚ〕*n.* 龍蝦
2. onion〔'ʌnjən〕*n.* 洋葱　　5. *in season* 正當時令的
6. *cut down on* 減少（份量）　　7. noodle〔'nudl〕*n.* 麵條（常用 *pl.*）
dip *v.* 浸　sauce〔sɔs〕*n.* 調味汁；醬
9. spinach〔'spɪnɪdʒ〕*n.* 菠菜　　10. carrot〔'kærət〕*n.* 紅蘿蔔
11. cabbage〔'kæbɪdʒ〕*n.* 甘藍菜　　12. entrails〔'ɛntrəlz, 'ɛntrelz〕*n.* 內臟
relish〔'rɛlɪʃ〕*n.* 美味；興味

20. Coffee, Tea & Cigarettes
咖啡、茶和香煙

1. **A**: How long is it since you gave up smoking?
   你戒煙有多久了?

   B: I haven't smoked a single cigarette for three years.
   我一根煙不抽已經有三年了。

2. **A**: How many did you smoke a day?
   你一天抽幾支煙?

   B: I used to smoke about 30 a day.
   我習慣一天抽 30 來支。

3. **A**: How much coffee do you drink?
   你喝多少咖啡?

   B: I suppose I drink three or four cups a day when I'm at work.
   我想我在工作時,一天喝三杯或四杯。

4. I used to drink it with a lot of cream, but now I prefer it black.
   我以前喝都加很多**奶精**,但是我現在喜歡喝不加的。

5. I know it isn't good for me, so I drink it weak — what we call American style.
   我知道那對我不好,所以我喝淡的—— 就是我們所謂的美國式。

6. Blue Mountain has the richest, most satisfying taste.
   藍山有最濃、最令人滿意的味道。

7. Because of the stimulant, caffeine, in coffee and tea, you may drink a cup of coffee or tea before you go to bed, and be unable to fall asleep. 由於咖啡和茶裏面含有刺激物──咖啡因，你在睡前喝杯咖啡或茶，可能睡不著覺。

8. For aroma and flavor, I think you can't beat Ceylon teas. 就香氣和味道來說，我想什麼也比不過錫蘭茶。

9. After a Chinese meal a cup of green tea is perfect; it really refreshes your mouth. 吃過中餐後，來一杯綠茶很棒；那眞能讓你口齒清爽。

10. With good Taiwanese tea you can enjoy three things : the taste, the fragrance and then the aftertaste. 有了上好的台灣茶，你可以有三種享受：味道、香氣、和餘味。

11. I haven't got the willpower to give up, and so I'm still a heavy smoker. 我還沒有戒掉的意志力，因此我仍然是個大煙槍。

12. I've cut the number of cigarettes I smoke by half. 我已經把煙量減半。

13. I only smoke cigarettes with a low nicotine content. 我只抽尼古丁含量低的香煙。

Note ──────────

4. black 咖啡中未加奶精或糖　　7. stimulant〔'stɪmjələnt〕*n.* 刺激物
caffeine〔'kæfiɪn,'kæfin〕*n.* 咖啡鹼；茶精
8. aroma〔ə'romə〕*n.* 香氣　10. fragrance〔'fregrəns〕*n.* 香氣
aftertaste 餘味　13. nicotine〔'nɪkə,tin , -tɪn〕*n.* 尼古丁
content〔'kɑntɛnt , kən'tɛnt〕*n.* 含量

公司機構的單位與職稱

Head Office：Main Office；HQ 總公司
～Branch（Office）～分公司
～Office ～營業處
～Plant；～Factory ～工廠
～Laboratory；～Research Institute ～研究室
～Department ～部
～Section ～課

Secretary 秘書
Public Relations 公共關係
Publicity 宣傳
General Affairs 總務；庶務
Files 文書
Finance 財務
Accounting；Accounts 會計
Legal；Law 法務
Personnel 人事
Management；Administrative 管理
Planning 企畫
Research & Development；R&D 研究開發
Research 調查
Technical 技術

Business 營業
Sales；Marketing and Sales 銷售
Production；Manufacturing 製造
Foreign Trade 貿易
Foreign 國外
Overseas 海外
Export 輸出
Import 輸入

President 董事長
Director 董事
Managing Director 常務董事
Auditor 稽查員
Advisor 顧問
Special Advisor 特別顧問
General Manager，～Department ～部總經理
Manager，～Department ～部經理
Assistant Manager，～Department ～部副經理
Manager，～Section ～課長
Assistant Manager，～Section ～股長

II. 公司・工作

21.Trading Company
貿易公司

1. **A**: What sort of company do you work for ?
   你在什麼公司工作？

   B: I work for a trading company.
   我在一家貿易公司工作。

2. **A**: How big is your company ?
   你們公司有多大？

   B: Our company has more than a hundred employees. It is one of the largest trading companies in Taiwan.
   我們公司有 100 多人，是台灣的一家大貿易公司。

3. **A**: What's your position ?
   你的職位是什麼？

   B: I'm a section head in the foodstuffs division.
   我是食品部的一個課長。

4. My work has always been in the field of hardware.
   我的工作一直在五金的範圍。

5. Before my present post, I was manager of our Chicago office for five years. 在我擔任目前的職位之前，我當我們芝加哥辦事處的經理已經有五年。

6. Business was tough in the U.S., but at least it gave me a sense of achievement.
   在美國做生意很辛苦，但至少它給我成就感。

7. I did most of my business in English, and that helped my ability in the language a lot.

　我大部分的生意都用英文溝通，那對我的語文能力幫助很大。

8. Trading companies attract a lot of applications from new graduates.

　貿易公司吸引很多剛畢業的學生來申請工作。

9. We have had good results in our re-exporting operation.

　我們在再輸出作業上已經有很好的成果。

10. I am on a committee considering whether to go into the information industry.

　我是委員會的委員，正考慮是否進入資訊工業。

Note ─────────────

3. position 職位　foodstuff〔ˈfud,stʌf〕*n.* 食品

4. hardware〔ˈhɑrd,wɛr〕*n.* 五金器具；金屬類　section 課；股　division 部門　5. post 職位　6. tough〔tʌf〕*adj.* 艱苦的

9. re-export *v.* （將輸入品）再輸出

10. *be on a committee* 爲委員會之委員

22. Banking Institutions
金融機構

1. **A**: Which bank do you work for ?
   你在那家銀行上班？

   B: I work at Bank of America, Taipei branch.
   我在美國商業銀行台北分行上班。

2. **A**: How did you get the job ?
   你怎麼得到工作的？

   B: They tested my typing skills and English conversation ability.
   他們測驗我的打字技能和英語會話能力。

3. **A**: How long have you been working there ?
   你在那裏做多久？

   B: I joined right after graduating from college, so I've been in this job for 5 years now.
   我大學一畢業就進來了，所以現在已經在這個工作上做了五年。

4. I've done various jobs, but mostly I've been with loans.
   我做過不同的工作，但大部分都在做貸款。

5. A lot of us are from the same university, and this makes it easier for us to work together.
   我們很多人都來自同一所大學，這使我們更容易在一起工作。

6. With the expansion of the Taiwanese economy, more and more people are being sent to work abroad.

   隨著台灣經濟的擴展，越來越多人被派到國外去。

7. I'm due to go to London as our representative soon, and I'm busy getting my English up to a reasonable level.

   我預定很快就要到倫敦當我們的代表，現在正忙著把我的英文提高到一個相當的水準。

8. The Ta Tung bank forms the nucleus of a big group of trading, manufacturing, insurance and service companies. 大通銀行形成一個大的貿易、製造、保險和服務公司集團的核心。

9. Interests rates tend generally to move upward in periods of prosperity.

   在景氣好的時候，利率大致呈上升的趨勢。

10. A guidepost has been set to limit foreign lending by U.S. financial institutions.

    美國的金融機構為限制對外放款活動，已設定了一個指標。

Note

9. prosperity〔prɑs'pɛrətɪ〕*n.* 繁榮　　10. guidepost〔'gaɪd‚post〕*n.* 路標

23. Manufacturing
製 造 業

1. **A:** What does your company make ?
   你們公司做什麼？

   B: Broadly speaking, we make two kinds of things : electrical machinery and domestic electrical appliances.
   大致上說，我們做兩種東西：電機和家電製品。

2. **A:** What is your special field ?
   你專門做什麼？

   B: I'm in R and D (research and development).
   我是做研究和開發。

3. **A:** You work for a pretty big company, don't you ?
   你在一個相當大的公司工作，對嗎？

   B: It's one of the world's biggest manufacturers of electrical equipment, and we have offices in every major country. 那是世界上最大的電氣設備製造商，我們在每個主要國家都有公司。

4. It's three years since I started working with semi - conductors. 從我開始做半導體已經三年了。

5. Progress in semi - conductors is so fast we can hardly keep up with all the articles published on the subject.
半導體的進展很快，我們幾乎跟不上所有發表的論文。

6. Before I came to this company, I had been working with computers , and spent two years in California.
在我到這家公司來之前，一直在做電腦，並在加州待了兩年。

7. There are three dozen PhDs in my lab.
我的實驗室有 36 個博士。

8. If my work is going well I keep working until late at night without bothering about the time.
如果我做得很順利，就繼續工作到深夜，不管時間。

9. Sometimes I'm invited to submit articles to scientific publications abroad. 有時我應邀提出論文給海外的科學刊物。

10. Next April I'm due to go to Singapore as a technical adviser to an associated company there.
明年四月我要到新加坡的一家關係企業當技術顧問。

Note ──────────

manufacturing 製造（工業）　　1. *broadly speaking* 概括而言

appliance〔ə'plaɪəns〕*n.* 器具〔美〕（尤指）電化製品

4. conductor〔kən'dʌktə〕*n.* 導體　　semi- ～ 半導體

9. publication 刊物；出版　　article 文章；論文

24. Secretary
秘 書

1. **A**：What kind of work do you do?
   你做什麼工作?

   B：I work in the secretarial section of a company called Fu- hsing.
   我在一家叫福星的公司秘書處工作。

2. **A**：How many people work in your section?
   你們的部門有多少人?

   B：First there's the section chief, then two men and five women.
   首先是一個處長,再來是兩個男的和 5 個女的。

3. **A**：Who is your boss?
   你的老闆是誰?

   B：I'm secretary to the vice- president.
   我是副總裁的秘書。

4. I suppose I was assigned to the secretarial section because of my bright personality and the way I deal with people. 我想我被派到秘書處是因為我開朗的個性,和我的待人處世之道。

5. I studied filing and shorthand at business school, but they don't help me very much.
   我在商業學校學檔案和速記,但是對我幫助不大。

6. My typing speed is slow, but I won't make mistakes.
   我打字的速度不快，但是不會錯。

7. Your female **colleagues** think of you as something special
   if you're a secretary, but really you're just an assistant.
   如果你是個秘書，你的女同事會認爲你是個特別的人物，但實際上
   你只是個助理。

8. It seems that there are some progressive firms in Taiwan
   where women secretaries do the same work as in America.
   似乎在台灣一些進步的公司，女秘書做的工作和美國的一樣。

9. Male secretaries come into direct contact with administrative
   problems, and can develop worthwhile careers.
   男秘書直接接觸管理問題，並能發展有用的事業。

10. If I can get a good match, I'll give up my job and get
    married. 如果我能找到一個好伴侶，我會放棄工作而結婚。

Note ―――――――――――――

4. bright 明亮的；開朗的　　5. filing〔'faɪlɪŋ〕*n.* 檔案整理
shorthand〔'ʃɔrt,hænd〕*n.* 速記
9. worthwhile〔'wɝθ'hwaɪl〕*adj.* 有價值的；有用的　　10. match 配偶

25. Working Conditions (1)
工作條件(1)

1. **A** : What are your working hours ?

   你的工作時間有多長？

   B : From nine to five, with one and a half hours rest from noon to one thirty.

   從九點到五點，中午到一點半休息一個半小時。

2. **A** : Do you have tea-breaks or coffee-breaks ?

   你們有沒有喝茶或喝咖啡的休息時間？

   B : One of the girls in the office brings tea around in the morning, and at about 3 p.m.

   辦公室的一個女孩會在早上及下午三點左右送茶來。

3. **A** : How much is your year-end bonus ?

   你們的年終獎金有多少？

   B : We start with the monthly salary as a base, then add to it according to seniority.

   我們以月薪為基礎，按年資增加。

4. We hold a meeting once a month to evaluate results of the month's work, exchange ideas, and bring up suggestions for improvement. 我們每個月開一次會，檢討一個月來的工作成果，並交換心得，提出改進的建議。

5. Meetings are an effective way of making decisions and forming a consensus.

   會議是決定事情和形成共同意見的有效方法。

6. We have lunch on our own but the company gives us an allowance to pay for food expenses.

　我們中飯自行解決，但公司每個月有發伙食費。

7. At lunchtime, everybody eats the same food at the same tables in the company canteen.

　午餐時間，每個人都在公司飲食部的同一張桌子上吃同樣的東西。

8. I often go out for lunch with a few friends, and eat noodles or quick lunch ; occasionally I bring a lunch box to heat up at the office.

　我常和幾個朋友出去吃午餐，吃麵或快餐；偶爾也帶便當在公司蒸。

9. When I have guests, I take them to a coffee shop, where we can talk things over better.

　我有客人的時候，就帶他們到咖啡店，在那裏比較可以討論事情。

10. I work overtime several times a month.

　我每個月都加幾次班。

Note ──────────────

2. tea-break 〔英〕喝茶的休息時間
coffee-break 〔美〕工作中喝咖啡的略事休息
3. bonus〔'bonəs〕*n.* 紅利；獎金　year-end bonus 年終獎金
seniority〔sin'jɔrətɪ〕*n.* 年資
5. consensus〔kən'sɛnsəs〕*n.* （意見等）一致
7. canteen〔kæn'tin〕*n.* （工廠、辦公處等的）飲食部
8. quick lunch 快餐　10. *work overtime* 加班

26. Working Conditions (2)
工作條件(2)

1. **A**：What sort of welfare facilities does your company provide ?

   你們公司提供什麼福利設施？

   B：Recreation centers, nurseries and so on are run for employees and their families.

   有為員工及員工眷屬開辦的休閒中心、育兒室等。

2. **A**：How much time off are you given ?

   你們有多少休假？

   B：We get three weeks' holiday with pay a year, but a lot of people don't take the full three weeks.

   我們一年有三週的有薪休假，但是很多人沒有休滿三週。

3. **A**：How active is your union ?

   你們工會活不活躍？

   B：It isn't as active as unions in the West; for example, it would never organize a strike.

   不像西方的工會那麼活躍；例如不會領導罷工。

4. We are given an hour off for lunch.

   我們午餐休息一小時。

5. The company organizes field trips and sports meets for its employees every year.

   公司每年都會替員工舉辦郊遊和運動會。

6. The company provides labor insurance for all its employees, as well as a fine retirement policy.

公司替全體員工辦勞保，並有完善的退休制度。

7. Until I got married I lived in one of the company's blocks of apartments for unmarried staff members.

我住在未婚職員的公寓裏，直到結婚為止。

8. There is a company union, but it really shares the same aims as the management.

公司有工會，但事實上和資方目標相同。

9. Because I'm on the managerial staff, I'm not in the union.

因為我是管理人員，所以不在工會。

10. I'm not really sure how much we get paid for overtime.

我不大清楚加班有多少錢。

Note ————————————

1. recreation 休閒；娛樂　　nursery 育兒室　　3. union 工會
5. field 野外的　meet 競賽大會　　6. labor insurance 勞工保險
7. block （連在一起的一片）大建築物
8. management （與勞方相對的）資方
9. managerial 〔‚mænə'dʒɪrɪəl〕 *adj.* 管理的　　staff 全體職員
10. overtime 〔'ovɚ‚taɪm〕 *n.* 加班

27. Traveling to Work
通　勤

1. **A**： How much time does it take for you to commute?
    你通勤要花多久的時間？

   B： From home to the office it takes me about an hour altogether.
    從家裏到公司大概總共要一小時。

2. **A**： How do you travel?
    你怎麼去？

   B： I walk for 10 minutes to the station, then take a train for 20 minutes, and then there's a 30-minute ride on the bus. 我走十分鐘到車站，然後坐二十分鐘火車，再搭三十分鐘的公車。

3. **A**： How does your commuting time compare with other people's?
    你通勤的時間和別人比起來怎樣？

   B： An hour is relatively good; nowadays there are a lot of people who take an hour and a half or so.
    一小時是相當不錯的；因為很多人要差不多一個半小時。

4. The high price of land and housing forces people to live further out of the city.
    土地和住宅的高價迫使人們住得更遠離市區。

5. The bus I am waiting for takes a long time to get here.

我等的那路車要很久才來。

6. I have to transfer buses so I spend twice as much for the bus everyday.

我要轉車，所以每天都比別人多花一倍的車錢。

7. During rush hour, the traffic jams block the roads for half an hour.

在尖峯時間，路上的交通會阻塞半小時。

8. My house is not far from the office, so I always ride my bicycle to work.

我家離公司不遠，所以我都騎腳踏車上班。

9. I have a car, but the congested roads and the parking problem mean I can't use it for getting to and from work. 我有一部車，但是擁擠的道路和停車問題就使我無法用車子往返上班。

10. The trains home are relatively less crowded, and I can read the evening paper or have a little sleep.

回家的火車比較不擠，我就可以看晚報或小睡一會。

Note ───────

1. commute〔kə'mjut〕*v.* 通勤　　4. housing〔'hauzɪŋ〕*n.* 住宅
6. transfer〔træns'fɚ〕*v.* 換車；移轉　　7. traffic jam 交通阻塞
block 堵塞　　9. congested〔kən'dʒɛstɪd〕*adj.* 擁塞的

28. Business Trips
商務旅行

1. **A**：Where does your company send you?
   你們公司派你到那裏?

   B：So far I've only been on trips inside Taiwan, but I'm going to be sent abroad next year.
   到目前爲止,我只有在台灣出過差,但是明年就要被派到國外。

2. **A**：How often do you travel on business?
   你多久出差一次?

   B：In my job as a sales engineer, I'm on the road about one week in every four.
   以我銷售工程師的工作,大約每四週就有一週在旅行。

3. **A**：What sort of expenses do you get?
   你有那些出差費?

   B：We have our fares and accommodations paid, plus a small daily allowance.
   我們有交通費和住宿費,再加一點每日津貼。

4. I often have to go and visit our suppliers and agents in different parts of the country.
   我經常得去拜訪全國各地的供應商和代理商。

5. I've just got back from Southeast Asia, where we're having a sales drive.
   我剛從東南亞回來,我們正在那裏做銷售活動。

6. One of my ambitions is to become our resident representative in Europe.

   我的抱負之一是成爲我們歐洲的駐外代表。

7. Because I'm in the accounts department, I rarely get the
   opportunity to make business trips.

   因爲我在會計部門，所以很少有商務旅行的機會。

8. Although we use things like telephones, telex and letters
   a lot, I still think face-to-face communication is important.

   雖然我們常常用電話、電報和書信等東西，但我仍然認爲面對面的
   溝通很重要。

9. My wife doesn't understand why I have to travel so much,
   and she is always complaining about it.

   我太太不了解我爲什麼要常常旅行，一直在抱怨。

10. I used to make a small profit on my travel allowances,
    but since the recession I haven't been able to.

    我以前會在旅行津貼上賺點小利潤，但是自從不景氣以後就不能了。

Note ─────────────

　2. sales engineer 銷售工程師

　on the road （推銷員）在巡迴各地途中

　3. expense （薪俸以外的）交際費；津貼

　　fare （火車、船等的）票價　　allowance 津貼

　4. supplier 供應商　　agent 代理商

　5. drive *n.* （募捐等）運動　　6. resident〔'rɛzədənt〕*adj.* 派駐的

　10. recession〔rɪ'sɛʃən〕*n.* 不景氣

29. Dressing
穿 著

1. **A**: What do you wear at work?
   你上班的時候穿什麼衣服?

   B: There's no uniform, but I have to wear a suit.
   沒有制服,但是我得穿一套西裝。

2. **A**: Where do you have your suits made?
   你衣服在那裏做的?

   B: I used to get them made at a tailor, but now I buy them ready-made.
   我以前都在西裝店做,但現在我買現成的。

3. **A**: Do you wear dresses?
   你穿不穿洋裝?

   B: I seldom do because wearing dresses is so inconvenient unless it's for a formal occasion.
   我很少穿,穿洋裝不方便,除非是在正式的場合。

4. Because you may sometimes have to entertain guests as a secretary, it's necessary to dress more formally.
   當女秘書因為有時候要接待客人,所以得穿正式一點。

5. There's a kind of unwritten law about what to wear.
   關於穿什麼有種不成文法。

6. Recently more people have taken to wearing jackets or blazers.
   最近有更多人開始穿夾克或運動衣。

7. You might think gray is dull, but I think it suits me.

　你也許會認爲灰色很沈悶，但我認爲我適合。

8. Even in the summer when it's hot and humid, I have to keep my jacket on.

　甚至在夏天又熱又濕的時候，我還是得穿夾克。

9. When I'm not at work I wear casual clothes in bright colors, just for a change.

　我不上班的時候就穿鮮豔的便服，只想來點變化。

10. Young people seem to have the knack of wearing the right clothes.

　年輕人似乎有穿好衣服的竅門。

11. I'd much rather buy expensive but good quality clothing, because it is not only nice but lasts a long time.

　我寧願買貴而質料好的衣服，因爲它既好又耐穿。

12. I like to buy imported accessories like cufflinks.

　我喜歡買像鏈扣之類進口的配件。

Note ────

　1. suit 一套衣服；西裝　　2. tailor 裁縫師；西裝店
　ready-made 現成的　　4. entertain〔,ɛntɚ'ten〕*v.* 招待
　5. unwritten law 不成文法　　6. *take to* 開始
　blazer〔'blezɚ〕*n.* 顏色鮮明的運動衣　　9. casual clothes 便服
　10. knack〔næk〕*n.* 竅門　　12. accessory〔æk'sɛsərɪ〕*n.* 附件
　cuff〔kʌf〕*n.* 袖口　　～link 男子襯衫袖的鏈扣

30.Introducing a Third Person
介紹第三者

1. **A**: Is this a friend of yours ?
   這是你的朋友嗎？

   B: Yes, this is Wei-ch'iang Lin ; we were at school together.
   是的，這是林偉強，我們唸同一個學校。

2. **A**: Could you introduce me to this young lady, please ?
   請你代我向這位小姐介紹好嗎？

   B: Of course. Mr. Smith, this is Ai-ch'in Yuan ; Ai-ch'in Yuan, Mr. Smith from Los Angeles.
   當然。史密斯先生，這是袁愛琴；袁愛琴，這是洛杉磯來的史密斯先生。

3. **A**: I don't think I've met this gentleman before.
   我想我沒見過這位先生。

   B: Oh, I'm sorry, I should have introduced you earlier.
   喔，抱歉，我早該為你們介紹。

4. I'd like you to meet my immediate boss, Mr. Wang.
   我想讓你見我的直屬上司，王先生。

5. Here's somebody I think you should meet.
   這裏有我認為你應該見的人。

6. Miss Wu here tells me she's seen you on TV.
   這裏的吳小姐告訴我她在電視上看過你。

7. I've been wanting to introduce you to Mrs. Brown for some time.

好久以來我就想把你介紹給布朗太太。

8. You haven't been introduced to Miss Chung yet, have you ?

你還沒有被介紹給鐘小姐，對嗎？

9. Come here and I'll introduce you to an old friend of mine.

來這裏，我跟你介紹我一個老朋友。

10. If you're not too busy, I'd like to introduce a guest of mine from our Canadian suppliers.

如果你不很忙的話，我想介紹來自我們加拿大供應商的一個客人。

11. I think it would be very useful for the two of you to get to know each other.

我想讓你們兩個互相認識是很有益的。

12. It gives me great pleasure to present to everybody here : Dr. Chin.

很榮幸在這裏向大家介紹：金博士。

Note ————————————

10. supplier〔sə'plaɪɚ〕*n.* 供應商

重要文學家名

Andersen〔ˈændɚsn̩〕安徒生

Byron〔ˈbaɪrən〕拜倫

Camus〔kaˈmy〕卡繆

Chekhov〔ˈtʃɛkəf, ˈtʃɛkɔf〕柴可夫

Dostoevski〔ˌdɑstɔˈjɛfskɪ, -jɛvskɪ〕杜斯妥也夫斯基

Faulkner〔ˈfɔknɚ〕福克納

Flaubert〔ˌfloˈbɛr〕福樓拜

Gide〔ʒid〕紀德

Goethe〔ˈgetɪ, ˈgɛtə〕哥德

Gorky〔ˈgɔrkɪ〕高爾基

Hemingway〔ˈhɛmɪŋˌwe〕海明威

Hesse〔ˈhɛsɪ〕赫塞

Hugo〔ˈhjugo〕雨果

Maugham〔mɔm〕毛姆

Maupassant〔ˈmopəˌsɑnt, ˌmoˌpaˈsɑ̃〕莫泊桑

Melville〔ˈmɛlvɪl〕梅爾威爾

Molière〔ˌmolɪˈɛr〕莫里哀

Pushkin〔ˈpʊʃkɪn〕普希金

Remarque〔rəˈmɑrk〕雷馬克

Sartre〔ˈsɑrtrə〕沙特

Shakespeare〔ˈʃeksˌpɪr〕莎士比亞

Steinbeck〔ˈstaɪnbɛk〕史坦貝克

Stendhal〔stɑ̃ˈdɑl〕斯當達爾

Tolstoy〔ˈtɑlstɔɪ〕托爾斯泰

Turgenev, -niev, -nyev〔tʊrˈgɛnjɪf, tʊrˈgenjɪf〕屠格涅夫

III. 興趣・運動

31. Reading
讀　書

1. **A**: How much reading do you do?

   你看多少書？

   B: I'm a regular bookworm, I get through two or three books a week.

   我是個標準的書蟲，每個禮拜會看完2、3本書。

2. **A**: What do you like to read?

   你喜歡看什麼？

   B: I'll read anything I can get my hands on, but I enjoy detective fiction best.

   我只要手裏有，什麼都看，但是我最喜歡看偵探小說。

3. **A**: What are you reading now?

   你現在在看什麼？

   B: It's a historical novel that was reviewed in the papers the other day.

   前幾天在報上有評論的歷史小說。

4. When I was in college I read a lot of French literature, especially existentialists like Sartre and Camus.

   我大學的時候看了很多法國文學，尤其是存在主義的，像沙特和卡繆。

5. I've read some of Hemingway's short stories in translation, but I'd rather read them in the original.

   我讀了一些翻譯的海明威的短篇故事，但是我寧願看原著。

6. Chin-yung's swordsmen novels can make me read day and night with no thought for eating or sleeping.

　　金庸的武俠小說可以讓我看得廢寢忘食。

7. My wife borrows a lot of romances and travelogs from the municipal library.

　　我太太從市立圖書館借了很多愛情小說和遊記。

8. My children spend too much time reading trashy comics.

　　我的小孩花太多時間看沒有價值的漫畫。

9. I can't go to sleep without doing a few minutes' reading.

　　我不看幾分鐘書就無法入睡。

10. You can buy books at the book exhibit for 20% off, but it is even cheaper when a publishing company is on the verge of bankruptcy. Sometimes it'll be 40% off or more.

　　在書展買書可以打八折；但是在出版社快倒閉時，書賣得更便宜，可以打到六折以下。

Note ────────────

1. bookworm 書蟲；書呆子　　4. existentialist〔,ɛgzɪs'tɛnʃəlɪst〕*n.* 存在主義者

6. swordsman〔'sordzmən, 'sɔr-〕*n.* 武士；劍客（*pl.* ─men）

7. municipal〔mju'nɪsəpl̩〕*adj.* 市的

romance〔'romæns〕*n.* 戀愛故事；幻想小說

travelog(ue)〔'trævə,lɔg , -,lag〕*n.* 遊記

8. trashy〔'træʃɪ〕*adj.* 無價值的

comics〔'kamɪks〕*n.* 漫畫

10. exhibit〔ɪg'zɪbɪt〕*n.* 展示會　　*on the verge of* 快要

32. Newspapers & Magazines
報章雜誌

1. **A :** Which newspapers do you get?
   你訂什麼報紙?

   B : I get two papers, the China Times News and the United Daily News.
   我訂兩種報紙,中國時報和聯合報。

2. **A :** Do you subscribe to the morning or the evening paper?
   你訂早報還是晚報?

   B : I have a subscription for each.
   我兩種都各訂一分。

3. **A :** What part of the paper do you read first?
   你最先看報紙的那個部分?

   B : I glance at the front page headlines, and then I turn straight to the readers' letters.
   我先瞥一下頭版的標題,然後直接看讀者投書。

4. I read my morning paper from cover to cover on the journey to work.
   我在上班的路上把我的早報從頭到尾看完。

5. I don't like people reading my paper over my shoulder.
   我不喜歡有人在我後面看我看的報紙。

6. After I come to work, I glance at a few special dailies.

我到公司後，就瀏覽一些專門的日報。

7. I feel the sensationalism of sex and violence in the newspaper has bad effects on society.

我覺得報紙渲染色情與暴力，對社會會有不良的影響。

8. I'm afraid I'm rather slow at reading English language papers.

恐怕我看英文報紙很慢。

9. It seems to me that one reason why weekly news magazines don't sell so well is that all the news is covered in the daily papers.

我看週刊賣得不好的一個原因是，所有的新聞都包括在日報裏了。

10. I don't subscribe to any weekly or monthly magazines, but I buy them occasionally at newsstands.

我不訂任何週刊或月刊，但是偶爾會到書報攤上買。

Note —————————

1. get〔口〕訂購（報紙、雜誌等） 2. subscribe〔səb'skraɪb〕*v.* 訂閱
morning paper 早報 evening paper；afternooner 晚報
3. headline〔'hɛd,laɪn〕*n.*（報紙雜誌上的）標題
4. *from cover to cover* 從首頁到最後一頁 6. daily 日報
7. sensationalism〔sɛn'seʃənl,ɪzəm〕*n.* 激情的方法；煽情主義
10. newsstand 書報攤

33. TV
電 視

1. **A**: What kind of television have you got ?
   你有什麼電視機 ?

   B: It's a color set, of course, with remote control.
   當然是彩色電視機，有遙控裝置。

2. **A**: How many channels do you have in Taiwan ?
   在台灣有多少頻道 ?

   B: Three, TTV, CTV and CTS.
   三個，台視、中視和華視。

3. **A**: What's your favorite program ?
   你最喜歡的是什麼節目 ?

   B: I haven't got a single favorite, but I prefer more intellectual programs.
   我沒有一個最喜歡的，不過比較喜歡知識性的節目。

4. I like watching TV movies and series.
   我喜歡看電視長片和影集。

5. My wife is a typical soap opera addict.
   我太太是標準的連續劇迷。

6. Our children glue their eyes to the set when cartoons come on.
   電視上在演卡通的時候，我們的小孩眼睛都盯在電視機上。

7. At peak hours, we often fight over which channel to have on.
在黃金時段，我們經常會爲了看那一台而爭吵。

8. I really ought to watch less, and read more.
我眞該少看一點，多讀一點。

9. It's easy to say that you watch too much TV, but you still keep on doing it.
你很容易說電視看太多了，但是你仍然繼續看。

10. It's best to pick and choose when watching TV so as not to waste time.
電視節目最好選擇性地看，以免浪費時間。

Note

1. set 〔視〕電視機
2. channel〔'tʃænl̩〕 *n.* 頻道　　TTV 台視 (Taiwan Television Enterprise)
4. series〔'siriz〕*n.* 影集　　　CTC 中視 (China Television Co. Ltd)
　　　　　　　　　　　　　　　CTS 華視 (Chinese Television System)
5. soap opera 〔美〕(電視、廣播的) 連續劇 (通常以傷感或鬧劇的方式處理個人或家庭的問題，以前常由肥皂製造商提供)
addict〔ə'dɪkt〕*n.* 耽溺於某種嗜好者　　6. glue〔glu〕*v.* 黏；集中
7. peak 尖峯

34.Radio
收 音 機

1. **A :** Do you usually listen to the radio ?

   你平常聽不聽收音機？

   B : Yes, I keep the radio on almost all the time, even when I'm studying.

   聽，我幾乎隨時都讓收音機開著，連唸書的時候也一樣。

2. **A :** Is your radio a good one ?

   你的收音機好嗎？

   B : It's not bad. It has a stereo, there's no noise, and there's also an alarm clock.

   很不錯，有立體音響，沒有雜音，還附一個鬧鐘。

3. **A :** Which programs do you listen to ?

   你聽什麼節目？

   B : I listen to music programs, both classical and pop music.

   我聽音樂節目，古典和流行的都聽。

4. Listening to the radio in your spare time is the most enjoyable thing in the whole world.

   閒暇時聽收音機是莫大的享受。

5. I never miss the pop music program on Sunday morning from 8：00 to 11：00.

   我從來不錯過禮拜天早上8點到11點的流行音樂節目。

6. I often use the radio just for listening to tapes.

   我通常是為了聽錄音帶才用收音機。

7. If I turn on the radio before I go to sleep, some light music lets me fall asleep easily.

睡覺前打開收音機，聽一段輕音樂，可以讓我容易入睡。

8. I only listen to language programs.

我只聽語文教學節目。

9. Usually you can hear all kinds of news on the radio before it's on TV.

聽收音機往往可以比電視更早知道各種消息。

10. ICRT has become a challenge in listening comprehension.

ICRT 成了聽力的一項挑戰。

Note ————————————

2. stero〔'stɛrɪo, 'stɪrɪo〕*n.* 立體音響

noise （收音機、電視等的）雜音　alarm clock 鬧鐘

3. classical music 古典音樂　pop music 流行音樂

4. spare time 閒暇　7. light music 輕音樂

10. ICRT 全名為 International Community Radio Taipei 台北國際社區廣播電台

comprehension〔,kɑmprɪ'hɛnʃən〕*n.* 理解力

35. Films
電　影

1. **A**：Do you go to the movies very often？
    你常常看電影嗎？

   B：I suppose I see about one film a month.
    我想我大概每月看一部。

2. **A**：Have you seen any good movies lately？
    你最近有沒有看什麼好電影？

   B：It's ages since I went to see a film.
    我已經好久沒去看電影了。

3. **A**：What kind of films do you enjoy watching？
    你喜歡看什麼電影？

   B：I like all kinds, as long as they're entertaining.
    我什麼都喜歡，只要好看。

4. When I was a student I was a real movie buff.
    我當學生的時候是個道地的電影狂。

5. I didn't miss a single French film that came to the theater
    near my lodgings.
    我沒錯過任何一部在我宿舍附近電影院上映的法國電影。

6. There's going to be an Italian film festival late this month.
    這個月末有義大利電影節。

7. A James Bond movie is on this week.

一部詹姆士龐德的電影在本週上映 。

8. I am taking my children to see some cartoons.

我要帶小孩去看卡通影片 。

9. Recently many movies have been screenplays adopted from novels.

最近有很多電影是由小說改編搬上銀幕的 。

10. I get the impression that because of TV, movie audiences are getting smaller.

我覺得因為電視的關係 , 使看電影的觀衆減少了 。

Note ──────────────

2. ages 〔口〕長時間 ; 久

3. entertaining〔͵ɛntɚˈtenɪŋ〕 *adj.* 令人愉快的

4. buff 〔bʌf〕 *n.* 〔美口〕(對某事有研究而熟悉的) 熱愛者

5. theater (ˈθiətɚ) *n.* 電影院

lodging 〔ˈlɑdʒɪŋ 〕 *n.* 住所 ;〔*pl.*〕出租宿舍

9. screenplay 電影腳本

36. Listening to Music
聽 音 樂

1. **A :** Are you a music lover ?

   你喜愛音樂嗎？

   B : Yes, I don't know what I'd do without my record
   player. 是的，沒有電唱機，我就不知道該怎麼辦了。

2. **A :** Who is your favorite composer ?

   你最喜歡那位音樂家？

   B : I don't have one single favorite, but these days I
   listen to a lot of Bach.

   我沒有最喜歡的一個，但這幾天我聽了很多巴哈。

3. **A :** What do you think about modern music ?

   你認為現代音樂怎麼樣？

   B : Some modern music is trash, but there are a lot of
   good rock groups, too.

   有些現代音樂是很沒營養，但是也有很多好的搖滾樂團。

4. I can't play a note myself, but I love listening to violin
   music.

   我自己一個音都不會拉，但是我愛聽小提琴。

5. Some people say that music has gone downhill since Bee-
   thoven, but I don't really agree.

   有人說從貝多芬以後音樂就走下坡，但是我不很同意。

6. Sometimes I wait in line for hours to get concert tickets.
   有時候我排幾小時的隊，等著買音樂會的票。

7. The other day we went to a piano recital by a promising young pianist.
   前幾天我們去聽一個有前途的年輕鋼琴家的鋼琴演奏。

8. It was a breath-taking performance, and we burst into applause as soon as the last note had been played.
   那是場驚人的演出，最後一個音符一奏完，我們就拼命鼓掌。

9. My record collection covers a comprehensive range of music from Bach to the Beatles.
   我的唱片蒐集包羅很廣，從巴哈到披頭的音樂都有。

10. I can't relax unless I have a record on.
    除非放唱片，否則我無法放鬆。

11. I could sit for hours listening to jazz.
    我可以坐著聽幾小時的爵士。

12. People who don't appreciate music are missing a lot.
    不懂音樂的人損失很多。

Note ——————————————

1. record player 電唱機　　3. trash〔træʃ〕*n.* (文學、藝術上) 無價值的作品
4. note〔樂〕音符　　5. downhill 下坡的 (地)；更壞
6. concert〔ˈkɑnsɝt〕*n.* 音樂會　　7. recital〔rɪˈsaɪtḷ〕*n.*〔樂〕獨奏會
promising〔ˈprɑmɪsɪŋ〕*adj.* 有前途的　　8. breath-taking 驚人的
burst into 突然發出　　9. collection 蒐集品
comprehensive〔ˌkɑmprɪˈhɛnsɪv〕*adj.* 包羅廣泛的

37. Playing Instruments
演奏樂器

1. **A :** What instruments do you play ?

   你彈奏什麼樂器？

   B : I can play the piano a bit, and I used to take trumpet lessons.

   我會彈一點鋼琴，以前學過小喇叭。

2. **A :** How good are you at the piano ?

   你鋼琴彈得怎樣？

   B : I would be much better if I practiced regularly.

   要是我定期地練，就會好多了。

3. **A :** How popular are traditional Chinese instruments ?

   中國的傳統樂器有多受歡迎？

   B : Quite a lot of people learn to play instruments like fiddle or flute.

   有很多人學胡琴和笛子之類的樂器。

4. I'm afraid my repertoire isn't very big.

   恐怕我演奏的曲目不很廣。

5. I learned how to read music, but I still can't sight-read.

   我學會看譜，但是我仍然不能不預習就演奏。

6. I just bought a guitar, and I'm learning how to play the basic chords.

   我剛買了一個吉他，正在學基本和絃。

7. Playing drums also **requires** learning ; you can't play them without knowing how.

打鼓也需要學，你不能亂打。

8. My wife wants me to buy her an electric organ.

我太太要我買一台電子琴給她。

9. I play the saxophone in an amateur jazz band.

我在一個業餘的爵士樂團吹薩克斯風。

10. My playing isn't really good enough for me to perform in public.

我的演奏還沒有好到可以公開表演的程度。

11. It would be nice to be able to sit down at the piano and just hammer out a tune.

能夠坐下來彈點曲子想必很好。

12. Let me play you one of my favorite tunes on the violin.

讓我為你用小提琴拉一首我最喜歡的曲子。

Note ————————

1. instrument〔'ɪnstrəmənt〕*n.* 樂器；儀器
3. fiddle〔'fɪdl̩〕*n.* 小提琴；胡琴
4. repertoire〔'rɛpə‚twɑr , -tɔrɪ〕*n.* 演奏節目
5. sight-read 不預習樂譜就演奏 (唱)
6. chord〔kɔrd〕*n.* 〔樂〕和絃
8. electric organ 電子琴
11. hammer 敲打　　tune 曲

38. Singing
唱 歌

1. **A**: Do you like singing ? 你喜歡唱歌嗎?

   B: Yes, I like it, but I don't have a good voice.
   是的,我喜歡,但是我的聲音不好。

2. **A**: What kinds of songs do you sing ? 你唱什麼歌?

   B: I prefer singing English songs, but if there are good popular songs, I sing them too.
   我比較喜歡唱英文歌,但是如果有好的流行歌,我也唱。

3. **A**: Which part do you sing ? 你唱那一部?

   B: I sang soprano when I was a child, but after I grew up, I have been singing tenor.
   我小時候唱高音部,長大以後就唱中音部了。

4. My voice is too low, so I often have to sing in a falsetto voice.
   我的聲音太低,所以我常常要用假音唱歌。

5. When I was younger I had quite a good tenor voice, and sang in our university Glee Club.
   我年輕時有不錯的男高音,並在大學的合唱團唱歌。

6. I only like to sing lyric songs and don't like songs with a quick rhythm.
   我只愛唱抒情歌,不喜歡快節奏的。

7. I started to sing English songs when I was in high school.
我從高中開始唱英文歌。

8. I don't dare sing aloud except when taking a bath.
我只有在洗澡時才敢引吭高歌。

9. The most terrible thing about singing is singing out of tune. 唱歌最怕走音。

10. People say that only fat vocalists can sing well, but I don't think that is quite right.
人們說只有胖的聲樂家才能唱得好，但我認為並不盡然。

11. Many middle-aged people like to sing Taiwanese and Japanese songs. My mother is no exception, in that just a karaoke can keep her happy for a long time.
許多中年人都喜歡唱台灣歌和日本歌，我媽也不例外，只要一部卡拉 O K 就可以讓她陶醉很久。

12. I can't sing a song for very long before I get tired of it. 我一首歌唱不了多久就會膩。

Note ─────────────

2. popular song 流行歌　　3. part 〔樂〕聲部
soprano〔sə'præno, -'prano〕*n.*（女性、少年的）最高音部　sing~ 唱最高音部
tenor〔'tɛnɚ〕*n.* 次中音；男高音　　4. falsetto〔fɔl'sɛto, -'sɛtə〕*n.* 假音
5. glee club 合唱團　　6. lyric〔'lɪrɪk〕*adj.* 抒情的
~song 抒情歌曲　　9. *out of tune* 不合調
10. vocalist〔'voklɪst〕*n.* 聲樂家　　vocal music 聲樂
11. karaoke 伴唱機；卡拉 O K（＝utaoke，日文原義分別為空桶；歌桶。）

39. Dancing
舞 蹈

1. A : Do you like to dance ?

   你愛不愛跳舞？

   B : Sometimes, if there's music playing.

   偶爾會跳，如果有音樂的話。

2. A : What kind of dancing do you like ?

   你都跳什麼舞？

   B : It depends on the music. For instance, if it's rock music I'll do disco, and if it's romantic music I'll do ballet.

   隨音樂而定，例如如果是熱門音樂就跳狄斯可，如果是抒情的音樂就跳芭蕾舞。

3. A : Do you really know how to do ballet ?

   你眞的會跳芭蕾舞？

   B : Not really, but I can imitate and practice on my own.

   不眞的會跳，但是可以自己模仿練習。

4. I don't like going to dancing parties because the atmosphere inside always makes you feel you're in a seedy place.

   我不喜歡參加舞會，裏面的氣氛老是讓你覺得你到了一個不正當的場所。

5. I like learning different kinds of folk dance. Folk dancing makes me feel energetic.

   我喜歡學跳各種土風舞，跳土風舞讓我覺得充滿活力。

6. I'm too inflexible. I think that's a big hindrance in dancing.

我的骨頭太硬，我想這是跳舞很大的障礙。

7. Aerobic dancing has become the craze recently. Many women who want to lose weight join aerobics classes.

最近盛行有氧舞蹈，有許多想減肥的女孩都參加有氧舞蹈班。

8. Modern dance has liberated dancers from the rigid forms of ballet and leaves a lot space for creativity for choreographers as well.

現代舞使舞者的肢體從古典芭蕾的束縛中解放出來，並使舞蹈創作有了廣濶的天地。

9. The Cloud Gate Dance Ensemble has given life to dance in Taiwan and also sparked appreciation for modern dance in Taiwan.

雲門舞集為台灣的舞蹈注入了生命，也使更多台灣人開始欣賞現代舞。

10. Don't say you can't dance. Just let your body move freely and you'll be fine.

不要說你不會跳舞，只要讓你的身體自由地動就好了。

Note ——————————————

2. ballet〔'bælɪ,bæ'le〕*n*. 芭蕾舞　　3. imitate〔'ɪmə,tet〕*v*. 模仿

4. seedy〔'sidɪ〕*adj*.〔口〕不正當的　　5. folk dance 土風舞；民族舞

6. inflexible〔ɪn'flɛksəbḷ〕*adj*. 剛直的　hindrance〔'hɪndrəns〕*n*. 阻礙

7. aerobic〔ɛ'robɪk〕*adj*. 氧氣的　aerobics *n*. 好氧性活動　craze 一時的狂熱或風尚

8. rigid〔'rɪdʒɪd〕*adj*. 僵硬的　choreographer〔,korɪ'agrəfə〕*n*. 舞蹈編作者

9. Cloud Gate Dance Ensemble　雲門舞集　spark　給與刺激

40. Watching Performances
看 表 演

1. A : Do you often go to see performances at the Sun Yat-sen Memorial Hall ?
   你常不常看國父紀念館的表演？

   B : I often keep an ear open for performance announcements and go when there's one I want to see.
   我經常在注意各種演出消息，遇到我想看的就會去看。

2. A : Which type of program do you usually watch ?
   你通常看那一類？

   B : I usually go to musical performances and also dance.
   我通常是去聽演奏，也看一些舞蹈。

3. A : Have you seen any performance you liked recently ?
   你最近有沒有看到什麼你喜歡的演出？

   B : My favorite was a piano solo by Vladimir Ashkenazy, and the performance of the New York Philharmonic was also incredibly good.
   我最喜歡的是阿胥肯納吉的鋼琴獨奏，還有紐約愛樂的演出也是棒極了。

4. I like the flowing style of the Lar Lubovitch Dance Company.
   我喜歡拉魯波維奇舞團流暢的風格。

5. Marcel Marceau's mime theater is rather thought provoking.
   馬歇·馬叟的默劇相當引人深思。

6. Last year I saw the performance of KODO at the Chinese Gymnasium and it was a great shock to me.

我去年在中華體育館看神鼓童的演出，受到極大的震撼。

7. Although you can see better if you use binoculars to watch dance, you often end up missing a lot of the action because the lenses are small and the movements change rapidly.

用望遠鏡看舞蹈，固然可以看得更清楚，但是因為鏡頭小動作變化快，所以到頭來常常會漏掉很多。

8. I don't really know how to appreciate Peking opera.

我不大會欣賞平劇。

9. I didn't know that the drama performances on the stage can have such rich forms and life until I saw the performance of the Lan Ling Theater Workshop.

看了蘭陵劇坊的演出，我才知道舞台上的戲劇表演可以有如此豐富的形態與生命。

10. What I hate most is the sound of coughing here and there during the pause between movements.

我最討厭在樂章之間的停頓中，有那些此起彼落的咳嗽聲。

11. Recently the vocalists of our country have worked very well together and put on several full scale opera performances.

國內的聲樂家近年來通力合作，推出了幾齣大型的歌劇。

12. You have to go early to buy tickets so you can get the best seat for your money.

買票要趁早，這樣才能以理想的票價買到最好的座位。

Note ————————————————

performance〔pə'fɔrməns〕*n*. 演出

1. announcement〔ə'naʊnsmənt〕*n*. 公告；通知

3. solo〔'solo〕*n*. 獨奏；獨唱

philharmonic〔,fɪlə'mɑnɪk,,fɪlhɑr'mɑnɪk〕*adj.* 愛好音樂的　*n.* 愛樂協會

incredibly〔ɪn'krɛdəblɪ〕*adv.* 非常地

4. flowing 流暢的

5. mime〔maɪm〕*n*. 默劇（演員）　theater 演劇；劇場

provoking〔prə'vokɪŋ〕*adj.* 刺激的

7. binoculars〔baɪ'nɑkjələz, bɪ-〕*n*. 雙眼望遠鏡（常作 *pl.*）

lens〔lɛnz〕*n*. 透鏡　8. Peking opera 平劇

9. workshop 工作場所；工廠　10. movement〔樂〕樂章

11. vocalist〔'voklɪst〕*n*. 聲樂家　*put on* 上演

41.Playing Chess
下　棋

1. **A**： What kinds of chess can you play ?

　　你會下什麼棋？

　B： All kinds, except for go. I can't play that very well.

　　我什麼都會，就是圍棋不行。

2. **A**： How do you play go ?

　　圍棋怎麼下？

　B： It's easier said than done. There are just two colors,
　　black and white. All you have to do is use your pieces
　　to surround the opponent's pieces and then take over
　　all of his territory. That's all. However when you
　　actually play, it can be very frustrating.

　　說來倒很容易，只有黑白兩種棋子，你只要用你的子去圍對方
　　的子，然後佔下他所有的地盤就好了，但是下起來就傷腦筋了。

3. **A**： How does Chinese chess differ from Western chess ?

　　象棋和西洋棋有什麼不同？

　B： The rules in both games are pretty similar but there
　　are some differences. Chinese chess, for instance, has
　　a cannon which can jump over another piece to attack
　　the opponent, but it doesn't have any pieces that can
　　move diagonally like the bishop or queen can.

　　兩種棋的下法差不多，但是有些不同，例如象棋有砲，可跳一
　　個子來打敵人，但是沒有像主教或皇后一樣可以斜走的棋。

4. When I was in college, there was a while when it was very popular to play gobang — whoever got five of his pieces in a row first, won.

我唸大學的時候有一陣子流行下五子棋──誰先把五個子連成一線就贏了。

5. In the autumn, when the evenings get longer, I like nothing better than to sit down to a game of Chinese chess.

在秋天，夜晚變長時，我最喜歡的莫過於坐下來和朋友下一盤象棋。

6. When I go around to my friend's house for a game we get so absorbed in it that I overstay my welcome.

我順道到朋友家玩棋，下得太專心，結果待過頭了。

7. My wife tells me I'm crazy to spend so much time sitting in front of a board.

我太太說我瘋了，才會花那麼多的時間坐在棋盤前。

8. Since my father retired, his main pleasure has been playing go with his friends.

我父親退休以來，最大的樂趣就是和他的朋友下圍棋了。

9. My son looks as though he's going to take after me, because he's started go already.

我兒子看來好像要跟上我了，因為他已經開始下圍棋。

10. He's only ten, but he knows some pretty advanced moves.

他只有十歲，但是知道一些很高明的招數。

11. We have a saying that you hate your opponents at go, but can't leave them alone.

我們有一句話說你下圍棋時討厭你的敵人，但是卻不能不理他們。

12. What I hate most while playing chess is having someone standing alongside who keeps telling you how to play.

我最討厭下棋時有人在旁邊指指點點。

Note ─────────

1. go 圍棋　　3. cannon〔ˈkænən〕*n.* 砲　　bishop〔ˈbɪʃəp〕*n.* 主教 diagonally〔daɪˈægənḷɪ〕*adv.* 斜地　　4. gobang〔goˈbæŋ〕*n.* 五子棋

6. *go round* 順訪　　absorbed 全神貫注的 *overstay one's welcome* 停留過久使人生厭　　7. board 棋盤

9. *as though* 好像　　*take after* 跟隨；像

42. Painting
繪　畫

1. **A** : What medium do you paint in ?

   你用什麼材料畫畫？

   B : I prefer to paint in oils, but I also enjoy drawing in crayon.

   我比較喜歡畫油畫，但也喜歡用蠟筆。

2. **A** : Is there a particular subject that you like to paint ?

   你有特別喜歡畫的題材嗎？

   B : I paint a lot of still lifes; I'm not very good at portraits.

   我畫靜物畫得很多；我不大擅長畫人像。

3. **A** : What do you get out of painting ?

   你從繪畫中得到什麼？

   B : I don't do it for fame or money — just for the pleasure it gives me.

   我畫畫不為名利，只為它帶給我的樂趣。

4. I take my sketchbook with me whenever I go away.

   我每次出去都帶素描簿。

5. I used to go to art classes in the evening once a week.

   我過去每週一個晚上去上美術課。

6. It's surprising how many businessmen and politicians are weekend painters.

眞令人驚訝，那麼多商人和政治家都是週末畫家。

7. The impressionists strike me as particularly interesting.

印象派畫家讓我最感興趣。

8. I think my style has been influenced quite a lot by Henri Rousseau, the 19th century French painter.

我認爲我的風格受十九世紀法國畫家亨利‧盧梭的影響很大。

9. As for Chinese painting, I prefer painting landscapes.

國畫我比較喜歡畫山水。

10. This is a picture I had exhibited at an exhibition of works by amateur artists.

這張畫是我在業餘畫家作品展中展覽過的。

11. I was offered quite a lot of money for it, but turned it down.

有人給這張畫出很高的價錢，但是我回絕了。

12. Whenever there's an exhibition of European paintings at a museum, I make a point of going.

每當博物館有歐洲畫展，我一定會去看。

Note ——————

1. crayon〔'kreən〕 *n.* 蠟筆 2. still life 靜物　 portrait〔'portret〕 *n.* 肖像
4. sketchbook〔'skɛtʃ,bʊk〕 *n.* 素描簿　 5. art 藝術；美術
7. impressionist〔ɪm'prɛʃənɪst〕 *n.* 印象派畫家
12. ***make a point of*** + ***V-ing*** 必定～

43. Photography
攝 影

1. **A :** What kind of camera have you got?

   你有那種相機？

   B : I've just bought a new XXX 35 — a single-lens reflex 35 mm camera, with a built-in flash.

   我剛買了台新的XXX 35 —— 一台單眼反射 35 厘米相機，內裝閃光燈。

2. **A :** Have you got many attachments for your camera?

   你替你的相機買了很多配件嗎？

   B : I've got a tripod of course, and a couple of extra lenses, but I'd really like one more for close-up shots.

   我當然買了三角架，和幾個特殊鏡頭，但還想要一個特寫鏡頭。

3. **A :** What do you like to take pictures of? 你喜歡照什麼？

   B : I'll photograph anything, but my favorite subjects are wild birds.

   我什麼都照，但最喜歡照野鳥。

4. I'm quite happy to spend hours waiting for a good picture.

   我很樂意花幾小時等一張好照片。

5. Photography is a really absorbing hobby.

   攝影真是個引人的嗜好。

6. I subscribe to a monthly magazine for amateur photographers.

   我訂了給業餘攝影家看的月刊。

7. A photograph I took of Mt. Ali won second prize in a contest. 我照的一張阿里山的照片，在比賽中得了第二名。

8. I sometimes develop, print and enlarge my own photographs, but usually I have them processed at a camera shop.

   我有時候替自己的照片顯影、沖印、放大，但我通常拿給照相館做。

9. Here's a photo of my wife and children, taken on vacation.

   這裏有一張我太太和孩子的照片，假期照的。

10. I used to take slides, but I changed over to color prints.

    我過去常照幻燈片，但是後來改照彩色照片。

11. A friend of mine has an 8 mm movie camera, and takes a few reels of film whenever he goes away.

    我有個朋友有一台八厘米的電影攝影機，他每次出去都照上幾捲。

12. My brother spends all his time filming his children with his video camera.

    我哥哥把他所有的時間都花在用電視攝影機，把他的小孩拍成電影。

Note ───────────

1. lens〔lɛnz〕*n.* 透鏡　built-in 內在裝置的　flash 閃光燈

2. attachment〔əˈtætʃmənt〕*n.* 附件　tripod〔ˈtraɪpɑd〕*n.* 三腳架

   lens〔lɛnz〕*n.* 透鏡　close-up〔影〕特寫

   shot〔ʃɑt〕*n.* 照片　5. absorbing〔əbˈsɔrbɪŋ〕*adj.* 吸引人的

8. develop〔攝〕顯影　print 沖印　process *v.* 使（彩色軟片等）顯像

10. slide〔slaɪd〕*n.* 幻燈片　print *n.*〔攝〕印出的相片

11. reel〔ril〕*n.* 一捲電影片　movie camera〔美〕電影攝影機

12. film〔fɪlm〕*v.* 拍成電影　video〔ˈvɪdɪ,o〕*adj.* 電視的

44. Collections
收　集

1. **A :**　Do you collect anything ?
　　　　你有收集什麼嗎？

　　B :　I collect matchboxes and strangely shaped stones.
　　　　我收集火柴盒和奇形怪狀的石頭。

2. **A :**　How big is your stamp collection ?
　　　　你集郵集了多少？

　　B :　At the last count it was just over 10,000.
　　　　上次算正好超過一萬張。

3. **A :**　How do you collect all your coasters ?
　　　　你所有的茶杯墊是怎麼收集的？

　　B :　Every time I go out for a meal or a drink I make sure
　　　　I bring a coaster home for my collection.
　　　　我每次出去吃飯或喝酒，都一定帶個茶杯墊回來收集。

4. I've built up a pretty valuable collection of foreign coins.
　　我集了相當珍貴的外國錢幣。

5. Sorting out all the picture postcards I've collected over the
　　past 20 years is quite a job.
　　要把我二十年來收集的所有風景明信片分類整理，實在是一番功夫。

6. First I sort them according to where they come from.
　　我先按它們來自那裏來分類。

7. My collection of matchboxes serves as a souvenir to remind me of places I've been to.

　 我收集的火柴盒成爲紀念品，使我想起我曾經去過的地方。

8. I'm in a butterfly collectors' club, and we exchange our spare specimens.

　 我參加一個蝴蝶收集者的俱樂部，我們交換多餘的標本。

9. Do you know anyone in your country who could send me any old photographs for my collection?

　 你知道你們國內有誰能送舊照片給我收集嗎？

10. I'd be happy to show you my collection of woodblock prints any time.

　 我樂意隨時給你看我收集的木版畫。

11. I'm always on the lookout for something to add to my collection.

　 我一向留意可以列入收藏的東西。

12. I ask my friends who go abroad to bring one back for me.

　 我要我出國的朋友帶一個回來給我。

Note ――――――――――

3. coaster〔'kostɚ〕*n.* 茶杯墊　　5. *sort out* 分類整理

8. specimen〔'spɛsəmən〕*n.* 標本

10. woodblock〔'wʊd,blɑk〕*adj.* 木版的

11. *be on the lookout for* 留意

45. Fishing
釣　魚

1. **A**： How popular is fishing in Taiwan?

    釣魚在台灣有多受歡迎？

   B： They say there are about 100,000 anglers; so you see
    that it is very popular indeed.

    聽說有十萬個釣魚的人；這樣你就可以知道它眞的很受歡迎了。

2. **A**： What sort of people go fishing?

    什麼樣的人去釣魚？

   B： Mostly men, from young boys to old men, and some
    women, too.

    大部分是男的，從年輕男孩到老人都有，也有些女人。

3. **A**： Do you fish in fresh water or in the sea?

    你是河釣還是海釣？

   B： I prefer the sea, myself.

    我自己比較喜歡海釣。

4. Often on weekends I take the bus to the coast and spend
   the whole day fishing.

    我常在週末搭公車去海邊，整天釣魚。

5. When I have a bit of money to spare I hire a boat and go
   out in that, but usually I fish from the shore.

    我撥得出錢的時候，就雇船出海去釣，但平常就在岸上釣。

6. I usually catch fish like mackerel and horse mackerel.
　我常釣鯖魚和竹筴魚。

7. Nowadays there's a lot of good fishing gear available : reels, fiber glass rods and so on.
　現在有很多好的釣具：線軸、纖維玻璃釣竿等。

8. There seem to be fewer fish around these days, perhaps because so many people go fishing.
　近來魚似乎比較少，也許是因為釣魚的人太多。

9. Once I caught ten bonitos in one day, but often I don't get a single bite.
　我曾經一天釣過十條鰹魚，但常常一條也沒上釣。

10. I landed a ten-pounder, but you should have seen the one that got away!
　我釣到了一條十磅的魚，但是你該看看逃掉的那隻！

Note ──────────

1. angler〔'æŋglɚ〕*n.* 釣者　　3. fresh water 淡水
6. mackerel〔'mækərəl〕*n.* 鯖　horse mackerel 竹筴魚
7. gear〔gɪr〕*n.* 工具　reel〔ril〕*n.* 線軸
fiber〔'faɪbɚ〕*n.* 纖維　～glass 纖維玻璃　rod〔rɑd〕*n.* 竿
9. bonito〔bə'nito〕*n.* 鰹　bite 魚之吞餌；咬
10. land〔lænd〕*v.*〔俗〕獲得

46. Gardening
園 藝

1. **A**：How big is your garden ?
   你的花園有多大？

   B：We only have a small patch in front of the house.
   我們只有房子前面的一小塊地。

2. **A**：What sort of things do you grow?
   你種什麼東西？

   B：I grow a variety of things, so that something is in bloom all year round.
   我種好幾種東西，所以一年到頭都有花開。

3. **A**：When is your garden at its best ?
   你的花園什麼時候最好看？

   B：It looks best in spring, when the plum and cherry blossoms are out.
   春天看起來最好，那時李花、櫻花都開了。

4. I've just planted some roses in my garden.
   我剛在我的花園裏種了一些玫瑰。

5. The lawn and the hedge need to be trimmed regularly.
   草地和籬笆得定期修剪。

6. In the back garden there's a persimmon tree which is laden with fruit in the late autumn.
   後院有柿子樹，深秋的時候結滿了果子。

7. My father loves potted plants very much.

　我父親熱愛盆景 。

8. He's going to enter his favorite miniature pine in a competition.

　他要把最喜愛的小松樹拿去參加比賽 。

9. Last year all my roses were eaten by bugs.

　去年我所有的玫瑰都被小蟲吃了 。

10. I'd like to grow vegetables, but there isn't enough space.

　我想種蔬菜 , 但是空間不夠 。

11. I'm looking for a plot of land near home where I could grow a few things like tomatoes and lettuce.

　我在找一塊家附近的地 , 好種些蕃茄、萵苣之類的東西 。

Note ────────────

1. patch〔pætʃ〕*n.* 一小塊地　　2. *in bloom* (花草) 在開花中

3. *at its*〔*one's*〕*best* 處於最佳時期　plum〔plʌm〕*n.* 李樹

5. hedge〔hɛdʒ〕*n.* 樹籬　trim〔trɪm〕*v.* 修剪

6. persimmon〔pə'sɪmən〕*n.* 柿子　laden〔'ledn〕*adj.* 結滿果實的 (接 with)

7. potted〔'pɑtɪd〕*adj.* 盆栽的　　8. miniature〔'mɪnɪətʃə〕*adj.* 迷你的

9. bug〔bʌg〕*n.* 小蟲　　11. lettuce〔'lɛtɪs , -əs〕*n.* 萵苣

47. Pets
寵 物

1. **A**: Do you have any pets ?
   你們有寵物嗎？

   B: We have a dog and two cats.
   我們有一條狗和兩隻貓。

2. **A**: What kind of dog do you have ?
   你們的狗是那一種？

   B: Our dog is a Scotch terrier ; her name is Hsiao-pai.
   我們的狗是蘇格蘭小獵犬，名叫小白。

3. **A**: Why do you call your dog " Hsiao-pai " ?
   你為什麼叫你的狗 " 小白 " ？

   B: Hsiao means " small " in Chinese, and pai means "white"
   in Chinese. He is a small white dog.
   Hsiao 就是中文的 " 小 " ，pai 就是中文的 " 白 " ，它是一
   隻白色的小狗。

4. Everybody in the family spoils him, so he's very attached
   to us.
   家裡每個人都寵牠，所以牠和我們很親。

5. He may be small, but with his loud bark he makes a good
   guard-dog.
   牠可能小了些，但是叫得很大聲，所以還是一隻好看門狗。

6. Twice a day we take him for a walk in the park.
   我們一天帶牠去公園散步兩次 。

7. When it's my turn to take him, I jog along with him, which
   kills two birds with one stone.
   輪到我帶牠散步的時候 , 我和牠一起慢跑 , 一舉兩得 。

8. Our cats are Siamese cats ; they're both male.
   我們的貓是暹羅貓 ; 兩隻都是公的 。

9. I have a pond with some golden carp.
   我有個池塘 , 裡面養了些金魚 。

10. Carp can cost thousands of dollars each, and some are
    pretty delicate, but mine were cheaper than that, and
    they're quite strong.
    鯉魚一隻可以貴到好幾千元 , 而且有的很瘦弱 ; 但是我的比較便
    宜 , 而且很壯 。

11. My daughter has a little bird in a cage, but it's often
    her mother or me who has to feed it and clean its cage
    out.
    我女兒在籠子裡養了隻小鳥 , 但是要去餵、要去清理籠子的常常
    是她媽媽或我 。

Note ————————

2. terrier〔'tɛrɪɚ〕*n.* 小獵狗　　4. *be attached to* 喜愛 ; 依戀

7. Kill two birds with one stone.〔諺〕一石二鳥 ; 一舉兩得 。

8. Siamese〔͵saɪə'miz〕*adj.* 暹羅的　　9. carp〔kɑrp〕*n.* 鯉魚
golden carp 金魚　　10. delicate〔'dɛləkət, -kɪt〕*adj.* 纖細的 ; 柔弱的

48. Shopping
購 物

1. **A**: How do you like shopping?
   你認為逛街買東西怎樣?

   B: I don't mind shopping for food and other daily needs.
   我不反對逛街買食品和其他日用品。

2. **A**: What do you think of big department stores?
   你認為大百貨公司如何?

   B: It's fun walking around them, but their displays are so good I'm tempted to buy things I don't really need.
   到處逛逛蠻有趣的,但是它們擺得那麼好,會誘我去買我不真的需要的東西。

3. **A**: How often do you go out shopping with your wife?
   你多久和你太太出去逛街買東西?

   B: She usually prefers to go shopping by herself, and I prefer it that way, too.
   她通常喜歡自己去逛街,我也比較喜歡那樣。

4. I like cooking too, so we often go out to the supermarket together.
   我也喜歡烹飪,所以我們常常一起去超級市場。

5. I never used to go shopping much until our baby was born.
   在我們的嬰兒出生之前,我從不習慣逛街買東西。

6. We look through the ads in the paper, and then go on shopping expeditions to the stores which are having sales.
   我們仔細看報上的廣告，然後出遠門到大減價的商店買東西。

7. Some big department stores sponsor art exhibitions.
   有的大百貨公司支持藝術展覽。

8. I enjoy browsing in the stationery store just around the corner. 我喜歡在轉角的文具店瀏覽。

9. When I was in Europe I went window shopping on Regent Street in London and the Rue St. Honoré in Paris.
   在歐洲的時候，我在倫敦的攝政街和巴黎的聖哈諾瑞街瀏覽櫥窗。

10. I got these shoes at a favorite shop of mine in Taipei Hsimenting.
    我在台北的西門町一家我最喜歡的店買了這些鞋子。

11. When my bonus comes out, I can't resist going on a shopping spree.
    我拿到紅利時，就忍不住要好好逛街買東西。

12. I have a feeling that I buy too much on credit.
    我覺得我記帳買了太多東西。

Note ——————————————————————

6. sale 大廉價　　expedition〔,ɛkspɪ'dɪʃən〕*n.* 遠征；探險
7. sponsor〔'spɑnsɚ〕*v.* 支持　　8. browse〔brauz〕*v.* 瀏覽
stationery〔'steʃən,ɛrɪ〕*n.* 文具　　9. window shopping 瀏覽櫥窗
11. bonus〔'bonəs〕*n.* 紅利　　spree〔spri〕*n.* 一段極放縱或活躍的時間
12. *on credit* 賒帳

49. Nature-Watching
觀察自然

1. **A**: What do you watch wild birds with?

   你用什麼觀察野鳥？

   B: I use a pair of high-powered binoculars so that I can watch them from a distance.

   我用一副高倍的望遠鏡，所以能從遠處觀察。

2. **A**: Where do you do your bird-watching?

   你在那裡賞鳥？

   B: There are a few good places to watch from quite near home.

   我家附近就有幾個相當好的賞鳥地點。

3. **A**: What do you get out of bird-watching?

   你從賞鳥中得到什麼？

   B: I feel as if I'm in direct contact with nature.

   我覺得就像在直接與自然接觸。

4. I film birds in their natural habitat.

   我在鳥的天然棲息地拍攝。

5. I've taken some good recordings of their songs.

   我把牠們的叫聲做了些不錯的錄音。

6. There's a swallows' nest under my roof at home.

   我家屋簷下有個燕子窩。

7. A lot of birds migrate to Taiwan in the winter, and sometimes you can see some really rare specimens.

許多鳥在多天遷移到台灣，有時候你看得到一些真正稀有的品種。

8. The best time to catch sight of those birds is the early evening.

看那些鳥的最佳時刻是在傍晚。

9. My son is interested in butterflies, and can identify dozens of different species.

我兒子對蝴蝶有興趣，而且能辨認數十種不同的品種。

10. I used to be an amateur astronomer and watch the stars through my telescope.

我以前是業餘的天文家，用望遠鏡觀察星星。

11. It's surprising how many different living things visit my garden.

有這麼多不同的生物來造訪我的花園，真令人驚奇。

12. I never get tired of looking at the trees and the way they change with the seasons.

我對樹和它們隨季節產生的變化從來看不厭。

Note ——————

1. power〔光〕倍率　binoculars〔baɪˈnɑkjələz〕*n.* 雙眼望遠鏡（常作 *pl.*）
from a distance 從遠方　　4. film *v.*〔攝〕拍攝
habitat〔ˈhæbə,tæt〕*n.* 產地；棲息地　　5. song（鳥等）鳴聲
7. specimen〔ˈspɛsəmən〕*n.* 樣品　　8. *catch sight of* 看見
9. species〔ˈspiʃɪz, -ʃiz〕*n.* 種　　10. astronomer〔əˈstrɑnəmə〕*n.* 天文家

50. Basketball
籃球

1. **A**：Which team are you for ?
   你支持那一隊？

   B：The Chinese team. Chun-cheng Hung is on it and I'm his loyal fan.
   中華隊，裏面有洪濬正，我是他的忠實球迷。

2. **A**：Do you know how to play basketball ?
   你會打籃球嗎？

   B：No I don't, I just like to watch.
   我不會打，只是喜歡看。

3. **A**：Do you understand basketball strategy ?
   你懂不懂籃球的戰術？

   B：I know a bit. There are basically 2 kinds of strategies, either group defense or one-on-one, and we can use them with flexibility.
   我知道一點，基本上有區域聯防和緊迫盯人兩種戰術，可以靈活運用。

4. I think basketball is the most suspenseful and exciting sport, especially when both teams are equally good, the winner frequently is not decided until the last few seconds.
   我覺得籃球賽是最緊張刺激的比賽，尤其是當兩隊旗鼓相當時，往往要到最後幾秒鐘才決定勝負。

5. I can't help but sigh with despair when I see the players on our side missing the basket so often.

　看到我方球員屢投不中，不由教人扼腕歎息。

6. The skills of America's Harlem Globe-trotters are out of this world.

　美國哈林籃球隊的球技真是出神入化。

7. In the past few years, my country has sponsored the Jones Cup Basketball Competition, and invited basketball teams from many countries to come compete in their basketball skills.

　我國近幾年來舉辦瓊斯盃籃球賽，邀請各國球隊來華切磋球技。

8. The physical build of Asian people is a born disadvantage in basketball.

　以東方人的體型來打籃球，在先天上就吃了虧。

9. Every Sunday afternoon I go to the elemetary school nearby to play basketball.

　我每週日下午都到附近的國小打籃球。

10. I heard that playing basketball makes you grow taller.

　聽說打籃球可以長高。

Note ───────────────

3. strategy〔'strætədʒɪ〕*n.* 戰略
flexibility〔,flɛksə'bɪlətɪ〕*n.* 彈性　　5. despair〔dɪ'spɛr〕*n.* 絕望
6. globe-trotter〔'glob,tratɚ〕*n.* 世界觀光旅行家
out of this world 出神入化　　8. build 體型

51. Watching Baseball
看 棒 球

1. **A :** Which team do you support ?

   你支持那一隊?

   B : The Chinese team. Their recent performance has been very good, and everyone agrees that they are likely to win.

   我支持中華隊,他們最近的表現很不錯,大家一致看好。

2. **A :** Do you often go to watch baseball ?

   你常去看棒球嗎?

   B : I go occasionally when there's a game on near home, but usually I watch it on T.V.

   我家附近有比賽時,偶爾會去看,但我通常看電視裡的。

3. **A :** What baseball games have you seen in the United States ?

   你在美國看了什麼棒球賽?

   B : I remember seeing the Yankees beat the New York Lions. It was the best game I had ever seen.

   我記得我看了洋基隊擊敗紐約獅隊,那是我看過的最好的比賽。

4. When my team is playing, nothing will take me away from the T.V.

   我的隊在比賽時,什麼也不能使我離開電視。

5. My wife laughs at me for cheering at the screen.
   我太太笑我對著螢幕加油。

6. I used to be a cheerleader for a group of fans.
   我以前是一群球迷的啦啦隊長。

7. Watching a live game is much more thrilling.
   看現場比賽刺激多了。

8. I will get up in the middle of the night to watch live
   coverage of baseball.
   我會在半夜起來看棒球實況轉播。

9. When the Republic of China's baseball team took part in
   the World Baseball Competition, I didn't miss a game of it.
   這次中華棒球隊參加的世界盃棒球比賽,我一場都沒錯過。

10. I don't do it myself, but a lot of office workers sneak
    out to watch baseball at coffee shops near where they
    work.
    我自己不這麼做,但是有很多公司職員溜到辦公室附近的咖啡店
    看棒球賽。

Note ————————————————

7. thrilling〔'θrɪlɪŋ〕*adj.* 驚險的

8. live coverage 現場轉播

10. *sneak out* 偷溜

52. Playing Baseball
打 棒 球

1. **A :** Can you play baseball ?

   你會打棒球嗎？

   B : Yes I can. I was on the baseball team even when I was in primary school, and while in college I also represented my school in competitions.

   會，我甚至在小學就參加了棒球隊，大學的時候也代表學校出賽過。

2. **A :** What position do you play ?

   你打那個位置？

   B : I play third base partly because I have a strong throwing arm.

   我是三壘手，多少是因爲我投球的臂力很強。

3. **A :** What are your batting figures ?

   你打擊數多少？

   B : My best was 0.300, which was not bad.

   最好是 0.300，還不壞。

4. I hit eight homers.

   我打了八支全壘打。

5. Very few people can hit my fast-curve ball.

   很少人擊得中我的快速曲球。

6. Sometimes I spend a whole afternoon practicing fielding, but I don't mind.

   我有時候花一整個下午練習守衞，但是我不在意。

7. I'm pretty good at stealing bases, and sometimes help to clinch a victory.

   我很擅長盜壘，有時候能促成勝利。

8. I'm getting a bit of a paunch, and may have to retire soon.

   我有點大肚子，可能很快就得退休了。

9. I think that the teamwork involved when we all pull together in a game helps us in our work, too.

   我認爲比賽中同心協力的團隊合作，對我們的工作也有幫助。

10. Every year, Taiwan sends a junior team, a junior youth team and a youth team to compete for the right to represent Asia in order to go to America and compete.
    The result is that we are always outstandingly successful.

    台灣每年都派少棒、青少棒和青棒爭取亞洲區代表權，到美國參加比賽，而且戰績輝煌。

Note ───────────

3. batting figures 打擊數
4. homer〔'homɚ〕*n*. 全壘打 (= home run)
5. curve ball 曲球　　6. fielding〔'fildɪŋ〕*n*. 守衞
7. clinch〔klɪntʃ〕*v*. 最終贏得　　8. paunch〔pɔntʃ, pantʃ〕*n*. 大肚子
9. teamwork 聯合工作　***pull together*** 同心協力

53. Tennis
網 球

1. **A** : How is your tennis coming along ?

   你網球打得怎樣？

   B : I just began. My serve isn't very good yet.

   才開始學，發球還發不好。

2. **A** : Who do you play tennis with ?

   你和誰打網球？

   B : I play with my wife, and I'm also a member of the company's tennis circle.

   我和太太一起打。我也是公司網球同好的一員。

3. **A** : Where is your nearest tennis court ?

   離你家最近的網球場在那裡？

   B : There are three in the park near where I live, but they're almost always occupied.

   我家附近公園裏有三個場地，但是幾乎總是有人用。

4. To play tennis you must first hit shots against a wall.

   打網球要先對牆壁練。

5. I've joined a tennis club, and have to pay pretty high membership fees.

   我加入了一家網球俱樂部，得付相當高的會費。

6. I feel that movements in playing tennis are very pleasant to watch.

我覺得網球打起來很好看 。

7. I prefer playing tennis on grass.

我比較喜歡在草地打網球 。

8. Tennis keeps you fit because you have to use every muscle in your body.

網球使你保持健康，因為你得用到身體每一部分的肌肉 。

9. A glass of beer tastes so much better after a good hard game of tennis. 一場艱苦的網球賽後，一杯啤酒喝起來棒極了 。

10. I've been feeling much more fit since I took up tennis.

我打網球後覺得健康多了 。

Note ─────────────────

1. **come along** 進行　　serve 發球

2. circle〔'sɝkl̩〕 *n.* 志同道合的集團

3. tennis court 網球場　　4. shot〔ʃɑt〕*n.* 打（球）

8. fit *adj.* 健康的

54. Golf
高 爾 夫

1. A： What's your handicap？

   你的差點是多少？

   B： It's been at 24 for a long time, and I don't seem to be getting any better.

   很久以來都是24，我好像都沒進步。

2. A： Do you manage to get plenty of practice？

   你有沒有設法多做練習？

   B： When I get the time I go and polish up some of my shots at the local driving range.

   我有空就到本地的高爾夫練習場去磨練球技。

3. A： How long have you been playing？

   你打多久了？

   B： Since my company moved me to Taipei.

   從公司把我調到台北開始。

4. I've become really enthusiastic, and have a game just about every week.

   我變得很熱衷，而且幾乎每個禮拜都來一場比賽。

5. Golf used to be an exclusive game, but now anybody can play.

   高爾夫球過去只有某些人玩，但現在任何人都能玩。

6. Membership fees at the big clubs are fantastically high.

大俱樂部的會費高得驚人。

7. I've joined a club which is quite a long way from home.

我參加了一個離家相當遠的俱樂部。

8. Unless I leave home early, I can't get a full 18 holes in.

除非我早點出門,否則我打不完十八個洞。

9. A group of golfers from my firm often go off together to play at different courses out in the country.

我公司裏一群打高爾夫球的人,常常一起到鄉間不同的球場打球。

10. Teeing off in the wide open spaces is a great release from the pressures of city life.

在寬濶的地方開球,很能消除城市生活的壓力。

11. Last spring I got a hole—in—one for the first time in my life.

去年春天我這輩子第一次一桿進洞。

12. Drinks after a game at the clubhouse bar — the nineteenth hole are fun, too.

比賽後在俱樂部的酒吧——高爾夫俱樂部喝一杯也很有趣。

Note ————————————

1. handicap〔'hændɪ,kæp〕*n.*〔高〕差點(打高爾夫時,爲優待劣者,從其實際桿數扣除 72 桿標準桿所剩下的桿數。)

2. driving range 高爾夫練習場　　*polish up* 改善

shot〔球賽〕打(球)　　5. exclusive〔ɪk'sklusɪv〕*adj.* 排外的　9. course 球場

10. *tee off* 開球　12. clubhouse 俱樂部的會所　nineteenth hole 高爾夫俱樂部

55. Watching Soccer/Football
看 足 球 / 橄 欖 球

1. A : Is there a particular soccer team that you support ?
    有沒有你特別支持的足球隊？

   B : I'm a big fan of the Taiwan University team.
    我是台灣大學隊的熱心球迷。

2. A : How is Taiwan's soccer ?
    台灣的足球怎樣？

   B : Can't say it's very developed, but the Mu-lan women's team is quite good.
    不能說很發達，但木蘭女子足球隊很好。

3. A : Have you ever been to a rugby match ?
    你有沒有看過橄欖球賽？

   B : I went to see Oxford play Cambridge a few months ago.
    幾個月前我去看牛津和劍橋比賽。

4. I like watching soccer for the speed and skill it involves.
    我喜歡看足球，它包含速度和技巧。

5. There's never a dull moment in a soccer match.
    足球賽裏從沒有沈悶的時刻。

6. I must say that I don't understand all the rules, but what I like about American football is the impression of great strength.
    我得說我不懂全部的規則，但是我喜歡美式橄欖球的一點，就是那強大的力量所帶來的感受。

7. When you see the players tackle each other you understand why they have shoulder pads.

當你看到球員互相絞扭時，你就會了解他們為什麼要墊肩。

8. I sometimes find myself cheering without realizing it.

有時候發現自己正在歡呼，但卻不知道是怎麼回事。

9. It may be a cold winter's day, but the excitement of a rugby game soon gets you warmed up.

那可以是個寒冷的冬天，但橄欖球賽的興奮會很快地讓你暖起來。

10. It seems to me that the secret of winning in rugby is teamwork.

我看打贏橄欖球的秘訣在於團隊合作。

11. If I had been the ref I wouldn't have given a penalty then.

如果我是裁判，那時候就不會罰犯規。

Note ————————————

1. soccer 〔美〕足球　fan（電影、運動等的）迷
3. rugby〔'rʌgbɪ〕*n.*〔英〕橄欖球
7. tackle〔'tækl〕*v.*〔橄欖球〕抱住；扭倒
pad〔pæd〕*n.* 墊子
10. teamwork〔'tim,wɝk〕*n.* 聯合工作
11. ref〔rɛf〕*n.*〔體育俚〕裁判（referee〔,rɛfə'ri〕的省略）
penalty〔'penltɪ〕*n.*〔競賽〕犯規的處罰；刑罰
* 橄欖球在美國稱為 football 或 American football，在英國稱為 rugby，rugby football 或 rugger；足球在美國稱為 soccer，在英國稱為 football 或 association football。

56. Swimming
游　泳

1. **A**： How long have you been able to swim？
　　 你會游泳有多久了？

　 B： I learned to swim when I was still in elementary school.
　　 我還在唸小學的時候就學游泳了。

2. **A**： How far can you swim？
　　 你能游多遠？

　 B： A dozen lengths of our local pool is no problem.
　　 我們那裏游泳池的十二倍長沒問題。

3. **A**： What's your favorite stroke？
　　 你最喜歡游什麼式？

　 B： I'm best at the crawl, but I enjoy the breast stroke, too.
　　 我最擅長自由式，但也喜歡蛙式。

4. The doctor told me to get more exercise, and so I joined a swimming club.
　 醫生告訴我要多運動，所以我參加了游泳俱樂部。

5. At first, I used to run out of breath quickly, but now I can just keep on swimming.
　 起初我會很快喘不過氣，但現在就可以一直游下去。

6. The municipal indoor pool is heated and stays open all year round.
　 市立室內游泳池是溫水的，而且全年開放。

7. Swimming gives me an appetite, but it also helps to keep
   my weight down.

   游泳使我有食慾，但也幫助我控制體重。

8. Our swimming club meets on Tuesdays and Fridays.

   我們的游泳俱樂部每週二、五聚會。

9. When I was a child we lived near the sea, and I used to swim
   a lot with my friends.

   小時候我們住在海邊，我常和朋友一起去游泳。

10. In the summer it's good to
    go to the sea, jump in and
    cool off.

    夏天去海邊很好，跳進去就涼快。

11. I took my children swimming
    in the sea last summer.

    去年夏天我帶小孩去海裏游泳。

12. I'm thinking of trying out
    some new styles of diving.

    我想試驗幾種新的潛水方法。

Note ─────────────

1. elementary school 小學　　3. stroke〔strok〕*n.* 一划；游法
crawl〔krɔl〕*n.* 自由式　breast stroke 蛙式
5. *out of breath* 喘不過氣　6. municipal〔mju'nɪsəpl〕*adj.* 市的

57.Skating
溜　冰

1. **A** : Do you know　how to skate？
   你會溜冰嗎？

   B : Yes,　I used to roller-skate；now I ice-skate.
   會，我以前穿輪鞋溜冰，現在我溜冰刀。

2. **A** : Do you skate at　the skating rink？
   你去冰宮溜嗎？

   B : Yes,　that's where I learned to skate.
   是的，我就是在那裏學會的。

3. **A** : Can you figure skate？
   你會不會花式溜冰？

   B : Oh, I'm far from being that good, I can only do a few turns, that's all.
   喔！我差得遠了，我只會轉幾圈而已。

4. Skating must be very exciting. It's too bad I can't skate.
   溜冰一定很刺激，可惜我不會。

5. Our favorite game at the skating rink is playing "dragon", in which a group of people skate together and someone who skates very well leads us from the front while he skates backwards.
   我們最喜歡在冰宮玩 " 接龍 "，那就是一群人連在一起溜，由一個很會溜的人倒退著在前面帶。

6. You have to be very careful when you skate on ice because you might bump into people and when you fall it's possible to get hurt by the ice skates.

溜冰要很小心，你可能和人相撞，跌倒時也可能被冰鞋割傷。

7. I like watching couples skating most of all for the harmonious and graceful dance movements.

我最喜歡看雙人溜冰和諧優美的舞姿。

8. Skating isn't very widespread ; almost everyone skating is young. 溜冰不大普遍，幾乎全部是年輕人在溜。

9. The young people who go to the ice rink come from all walks of life. Many are juvenile delinquents. I think it's better not to go too often.

去冰宮的年輕人份子很雜,有不少是不良少年，我想還是少去爲妙。

10. Taiwan's skating rinks are small, the ice is thin, and some have columns. The facilities are far from ideal.

台灣的冰宮場地小，冰層薄，有的還有柱子，設備很不理想。

Note ─────────

1. roller-skate *v*. 穿輪鞋溜冰　　ice-skate *v*. 溜冰

2. rink〔rɪŋk〕*n*. 溜冰場　skating ～ (室內)溜冰場　3. figure skating 花式溜冰

6. bump〔bʌmp〕*v*. 撞　　skates 溜冰鞋 (常用 *pl*. ; roller-～輪式溜冰鞋;

ice ～冰刀)　9. juvenile〔'dʒuvənḷ ,-,naɪl〕*adj.* 少年的

delinquent〔dɪ'lɪŋkwənt〕*n*. 犯過者

juvenile ～s 太保；太妹　　10. column〔'kɑləm〕*n*. 圓柱

58. Mountain-Climbing
登 山

1. **A :** What's the highest mountain you've ever climbed ?
   你爬過最高的山是什麼山？

   B : I've been up Mt. Jade a couple of times, but it isn't a
   difficult mountain to climb.
   我上過玉山幾次，但那不是什麼難爬的山。

2. **A :** What sort of equipment do you use ?
   你用什麼裝備？

   B : On difficult mountains we have to use ropes, pitons and
   so on.
   難爬的山我們得用繩子、鐵栓等。

3. **A :** Can you climb all year round ?
   你一年到頭都能爬山嗎？

   B : More or less, but we have to watch out for typhoons for
   these can cause landslides.
   大概可以，但是必須注意颱風，因為會引起山崩。

4. Mt. Ali isn't much fun on the way up, but sunrise from
   the summit is an incredible sight.
   上阿里山的路不怎麼有趣，但是山頂上的日出太美了。

5. I was on the first team to climb the north face of Mt. Snow.
   我是爬雪山北面的第一隊。

6. It is not always the highest mountains which are the
   hardest to climb.
   最高的山未必最難爬。

7. Before climbing it is best to be properly prepared, in case
   of any mishap.
   爬山之前最好有萬全的準備，以免發生山難。

8. I got caught in a typhoon and had to shelter in a cave.
   我碰上了颱風，得躲在洞裏。

9. It's easy to get lost on a mountain you don't know.
   在你不熟悉的山上容易迷路。

10. I set off early in the morning with my rucksack full of
    equipment and provisions for the climb.
    我一大早帶著裝滿爬山裝備和食物的背包出發了。

11. I'm not up to the steep slopes any more.
    我不能再爬真正的陡坡。

Note ——————————————————

2. piton〔'pitɑn〕*n.* 鐵栓　　3. landslide〔'lænd,slaɪd〕*n.* 山崩

7. mishap〔'mɪs,hæp，mɪs'hæp〕*n.* 不幸事件　　8. shelter〔'ʃɛltɚ〕*v.* 躲避

10. rucksack〔'rʌk,sæk〕*n.* 背包　　12. *up to* 能勝任

59. Hiking
遠 足

1. **A**: How do you spend weekends with your family?
   你和你的家人怎樣過週末？

   B: We often go out for picnics. 我們常去野餐。

2. **A**: Do you have to go far to find a good place?
   你得走很遠才會找到好地方嗎？

   B: There are some pretty pleasant places for a picnic an hour or two away by train.
   坐一兩個小時的火車就有很好的野餐地點。

3. **A**: Where do you like to hike?
   你喜歡去那裏徒步旅行？

   B: Along rivers, around lakes, up mountains — anywhere!
   沿著河，繞湖，上山——
   到任何地方！

4. I love the feeling of eating a packed lunch in the open air.
   我喜歡在野外吃便當的感覺。

5. When the whole family goes together we choose a safe, easy course.
   全家一起去的時候，我們選安全
   、容易走的路線。

6. Last winter vacation I went on the China Youth Corps' self-survival activity, which was a hike on the East Coast. It was very tiring but I was very happy since I saw beautiful scenery and was with my friends.

去年寒假，我參加救國團冬令自强活動的東海岸健行。走得很累，但是看到美麗的風景，又和朋友在一起，感到非常愉快。

7. Last weekend I walked to the Green Cloud Temple above Guanzihling in Chiayi county, stayed overnight there and came back the next day.

上週末，我走到嘉義關仔嶺上的碧雲寺，在那裏過了一夜，第二天回來。

8. For someone of my age walking up those mountain tracks is good exercise for his legs.

對我這個年紀的人來說，走上這些山路對脚是很好的運動。

9. My wife is interested in rural history and likes walking through little old country villages and towns.

我太太對農村歷史有興趣，喜歡走訪古老的小村鎮。

10. I think it's important for people like us in the city to come into contact with nature and the seasons.

我想對像我們這樣的都市人來說，和自然及季節接觸是很重要的。

11. Breathing the fresh air in the woods is said to be as good for you as sun-bathing ; you might call it "woodbathing."

在森林中呼吸新鮮空氣，據說和日光浴一樣好，你或可稱它爲 "森林浴"。

Note ───────────

hiking〔ˊhaɪkɪŋ〕*n.* 遠足；徒步旅行　　4. packed lunch 便當

in the open air 在野外　　5. course 路線

60. Driving
開　車

1. **A :** Why don't you drive to work ?

　　 你爲什麼不開車上班？

　　B : The roads in the city are so crowded it would take me much longer to drive than to go by train.

　　　在市區路上太擠，開車比搭火車要慢多了。

2. **A :** What make is your car ?

　　 你的車子是什麼牌子？

　　B : It's a Ford, and I've had it for three years now.

　　　福特的，我已經用了三年了。

3. **A :** How does your car perform ?

　　 你的車子用起來如何？

　　B : It's pretty economical in city traffic, and on the open road it will cruise at .60 m.p.h.

　　　在市區開相當經濟，在寬濶的道路上行駛，時速是 60 哩。

4. Gas is not cheap, and a long journey can be very expensive, especially if you have expressway tolls to pay.

　　汽油不便宜，開長途可能會很貴，尤其是你還要付高速公路的路費。

5. Because of the congestion, we make a point of leaving early whenever we go out in the car.

　　由於交通擁擠，我們每次開車出去一定早點走。

6. If we didn't take the expressways, we wouldn't get any-where.

   如果我們不走高速公路，那裏都去不了。

7. There are quite a lot of nice places within an hour's drive of where we live.

   有很多不錯的地方離我們住的地方只要一小時車程。

8. Next Sunday we're going to go on a driving tour around Tamsui.

   下週日我們要開車環遊淡水。

9. On the way we'll get out to stretch our legs and my wife will take over the driving.

   我們在路上會下車伸伸腿，換我太太來開車。

10. I've been driving for 20 years and have never had a serious accident ─ knock on wood !

    我開車開了二十年，還沒有過嚴重的意外──希望以後也不會發生！

11. My wife passed her test last year, but she intends to be what we call a paper driver, and never actually drive.

    我太太去年通過了考試，但是她打算當所謂的紙上駕駛，從不眞的開車。

Note ────────────

    2. make〔mek〕*n.* 牌子　3. cruise〔kruz〕*v.* 以最省燃料的速度進行　m.p.h ＝ miles per hour 時速～英里　4. toll〔tol〕*n.* 通行費　5. congestion〔kən'dʒɛstʃən〕*n.* 擁擠　10. *knock on wood* 敲擊木器以避凶；希望災禍不會發生

61. Travel
旅 行

1. **A**: Do you do a lot of traveling?
   你常常旅行嗎?

   B: I love it, and I travel as much as I can.
   我喜愛旅行, 而且儘可能旅行。

2. **A**: Where have you been?
   你去了那裏?

   B: I've been just about everywhere in Taiwan.
   我只是到台灣各地走走。

3. **A**: What's the nicest place you've ever visited?
   哪裏是你到過的最好的地方?

   B: That's difficult to say, but I can never visit Hsi Tou
   Forest Area too often.
   很難說, 但是溪頭我百去不厭。

4. Recently it has become popular for people in Taiwan to
   have travel agencies arrange tours for them abroad.
   最近在台灣的人盛行由旅行社包辦出國旅遊。

5. It's fun to meet new people in new places.
   在陌生的地方認識新面孔很有意思。

6. I enjoy traveling either by myself or with my family.
   我喜歡自己旅行或和家人一起。

7. Different places are worth visiting at different times of the year.

不同的地方值得在一年不同的時節去**遊覽**。

8. I've just come back from a tour of Japan.

我剛從日本旅遊回來。

9. We're planning to go on a package tour to Hong Kong.

我們計畫參加包辦旅遊去香港。

10. I'm quite a seasoned traveler, but I still find flying exciting.

我算是個旅行慣了的人，但我仍然覺得坐飛機是很興奮的事。

11. The farthest I've flown to is Los Angeles.

我飛過最遠的是到洛杉磯。

12. One thing I'd like to do is go on a Mediterranean cruise.

我想做的一件事就是乘船來一次地中海之旅。

Note ─────────

3. *can never*〔*not*〕～*too* … 再～也不為過

9. package tour （由旅行社提供而包括一切費用的）包辦旅遊

10. seasoned〔'siznd〕*adj.* 已習慣的

12. Mediterranean〔,mɛdətə'renɪən〕*adj.* 地中海的

the～sea 地中海　cruise〔kruz〕*n.* （船等）巡遊

go on a～ 乘船旅遊

62. Practicing Kung Fu
練 功 夫

1. **A** : Do you know any kung fu ?

   你會功夫嗎?

   B : Not really, but I've learned some before.

   不算會,但是學過一點。

2. **A** : What have you learned ?

   你學過什麼?

   B : I learned some karate for self-defense and I learned some shadow-boxing.

   我學過一點空手道,用來防身的;另外還學過一點太極拳。

3. **A** : What do you think of shadow-boxing ?

   你覺得太極拳怎樣?

   B : I think shadow-boxing can make you feel at peace. In addition to emphasizing matching the movements with your breathing, it is good for your health too.

   我覺得打太極拳可以使人心境平和,加上它注重呼吸配合動作,對健康也有好處。

4. I've forgotten everything I learned.

   我學過的通通忘了。

5. I do one set of shadow-boxing every morning after I get up.

   我每天早上起來都打一趟太極拳。

6. I feel the primary reason for practicing kung fu is for health reasons. Defense is of secondary importance and hurting others is absolutely unacceptable.

我覺得練武的首要目的在於鍛鍊身體，其次是防身，至於用來傷人是萬萬不可以的。

7. I've kept up my judo because it not only keeps me fit but also helps me to concentrate through meditation.

我一直在練柔道，因爲它不僅使我保持健康，而且也幫助我經由冥思來集中精神。

8. You don't look like a third dan in karate.

看不出你是空手道三段。

9. Recently, my mother learned Wai-tan kung, purely to benefit her health.

我媽媽最近在學外丹功，那純粹是用來健身的。

10. Chinese kung fu is magnificent and profound but it's unfortunate that a lot of it has not been passed down.

中國的功夫博大精深，可惜有很多已經失傳了。

Note ─────────────

kung fu〔ˌkuŋˈfu〕*n.* (中國) 功夫

2. karate〔kɑˈrɑte, -tɪ〕*n.* 空手道　　shadow-boxing 太極拳

6. *of secondary importance* 次要的

unacceptable〔ˌʌnəkˈsɛptəbl̩〕*adj.* 無法接受的

7. fit 健康的　　judo〔ˈdʒudo〕*n.* 柔道

meditation〔ˌmɛdəˈteʃən〕*n.* 沈思；冥想　　8. dan〔dən, dæn〕*n.* 段

63. Do-It-Yourself
自己動手

1. **A**： Are you handy around the house?
   你很會做家裏的活嗎？

   B： I can fix most things myself, if it's not too big a job.
   我能自己修大部份的東西，如果不太麻煩的話。

2. **A**： What sorts of things can you fix without calling some-one in?
   哪些東西你能自己修，不必叫人來做？

   B： I can do simple painting, carpentry and plumbing.
   我能做簡單的油漆、木工和修水管等工作。

3. **A**： What jobs have you done recently?
   你最近做了什麼？

   B： The other week I dug a pond for my children to keep goldfish in.
   上個禮拜我給小孩挖了個池子養金魚。

4. Our house needs a few repairs, and I'll have to get down to them soon.
   我們的房子需要修補，我得趕快動工。

5. There's so much to do I actually seem to work harder on my days off.
   有這麼多事要做，我休假時似乎工作得更辛苦。

6. The professionals often turn down the smaller jobs.
   專業人員常常拒絕做小工作。

7. If it has anything to do with cars, you can leave it up to me!
   如果是和車子有關的事，你可以讓我來！

8. Ever since I was a child I've enjoyed taking things apart
   and putting them together again.
   我從小就喜歡把東西拆開，再裝起來。

9. Our living room needs re-decorating, but I can't afford to
   have it done, so I'll have to do it myself, I suppose.
   我們的客廳需要重新裝修，但是我請不起別人來做，所以我想得自
   己動手了。

10. My wife wants me to put up some new shelves.
    我太太要我做幾個架子。

11. If I had some of the latest tools I've seen in the stores,
    I could finish everything off in half the time.
    如果我有在店裏看到的一些最新的工具，我可以在一半的時間內
    完成一切。

Note ─────────

2. carpentry〔'kɑrpəntrɪ〕 *n.* 木工　　plumbing〔'plʌmɪŋ〕 *n.* 修理水管等工作

4. repairs〔常用 *pl.*〕修理的工作　　*get down to* 處理

8. *take ～ apart* 把 (機器等) 拆開　　10. *put up* 建築；舉起

64. Daily Routine
日常事務

1. **A**：Are you an early riser？
   你早起嗎？

   B：On weekdays I have to get up at 6：30, but on Sundays I sleep late.
   我每天得六點半起床，但是星期天就起得晚。

2. **A**：What do you do before setting off for work？
   你去上班前做些什麼？

   B：After I've had a shave and eaten some breakfast there's hardly time for anything else.
   我刮完鬍子，吃點早餐後，幾乎就沒時間做別的事了。

3. **A**：What time do you get home？
   你幾點到家？

   B：If I go straight home, I can be back by seven.
   如果我直接回家，七點以前可以到。

4. I glance at the newspaper, and listen to the news on the radio.
   我瀏覽一下報紙，聽收音機的新聞。

5. We don't usually speak much over breakfast.
   我們通常吃早餐的時候不會說很多話。

6. Breakfast is sometimes the only time of the day when the family are all together.

有時候早餐是全家人唯一聚在一起的時候。

7. Just before leaving for work I water my plants.

我在臨上班前澆花。

8. My wife sees me off at the door.

我太太在門口送我。

9. When I get home, my dinner is waiting for me.

我到家時,晚餐已經替我準備好了。

10. I like to relax in a good hot bath.

我喜歡好好洗個熱水澡,鬆弛一下。

11. I'm afraid I don't have the energy to do more than watch TV.

恐怕我除了看電視外,就沒精神做別的事了。

12. We send the children to bed at nine, but often don't go ourselves until midnight.

我們九點送小孩上床睡覺,但自己通常要到半夜才睡。

Note ─────────────

2. *set off* 出發　　7. water *v.* 澆水　　8. *see sb. off* 給某人送行

重要音樂家名

Bach〔bɑk , bɑx〕巴哈

Beethoven〔'betovən〕貝多芬

Berlioz〔'bɛrlɪ,oz〕白遼士

Bizet〔bi'zɛ〕比才

Brahms〔brɑmz〕布拉姆斯

Chopin〔'ʃopæn , ʃo'pæn , ʃo'pæ̃〕蕭邦

Debussy〔də'bjusɪ〕德布西

Dvořák〔'dvɔrʒɑk〕德佛札克

Händel〔'hændl̩〕韓德爾

Haydn〔'haɪdn̩ , 'hedn̩〕海頓

Liszt〔lɪst〕李斯特

Mahler〔'mɑlɚ〕馬勒

Mendelssohn〔'mɛndl̩sn̩ , -,son〕孟德爾頌

Mozart〔'mozɑrt , 'motsɑrt〕莫札特

Puccini〔pu'tʃini〕普契尼

Ravel〔,rɑ'vɛl〕拉威爾

Rossini〔ro'sini〕羅西尼

Saint-Saëns〔sæ̃'sɑ̃〕聖桑

Schubert〔'ʃubɚt , 'ʃɪu-〕舒伯特

Schumann〔'ʃumən〕舒曼

Shostakovich〔,ʃɑstə'kovɪtʃ〕蕭士塔哥維其

Stravinsky〔strə'vɪnskɪ〕史特拉文斯基

Tchaikovsky〔tʃaɪ'kɔfskɪ , -vskɪ〕柴可夫斯基

Vivaldi〔vɪ'vɑldɪ〕韋瓦第

Wagner〔'vɑgnɚ , 'wægnɚ〕華格納

IV. 個性・信仰

65. My Personality
個　性

1. **A**: Would you say that you were an outgoing person?
   你認為你外向嗎?

   B: I think I'm rather on the shy side.
   我想我是比較內向的。

2. **A**: How would you like other people to see you?
   你喜歡別人怎麼看你?

   B: I'd like to be thought of as someone who can be trusted.
   我喜歡被看作可以信賴的人。

3. **A**: How do you get along with people with different characters from your own?
   你怎麼和與你性格不同的人相處?

   B: I try to adapt the way I act to suit them.
   我試著調整自己的行為方式來適應他們。

4. I think I'm reasonably cheerful by nature.
   我想我生性相當開朗。

5. I'm patient but firm in handling angry customers.
   我對付生氣的顧客很有耐心，但也很堅決。

6. My wife tells me I'm too much of a spendthrift.
   我太太說我太浪費了。

7. I like to be well-dressed, but not too conspicuously.

我喜歡穿得好，但又不太引人注目。

8. One of my big faults is that I don't pay enough attention to details.

我的一大缺點是，我不夠注意細節。

9. I overheard someone the other day saying that I was moody and unpredictable.

我前幾天無意中聽到有人說我陰沈、不可捉摸。

10. I may look dull and uninteresting, but you'll be surprised when you get to know me better.

我看起來也許呆板、無趣，但是你更了解我以後，就會很驚訝。

11. One aspect of my character that few people get to see is my bad temper.

我性格中很少人看得出來的一面就是脾氣壞。

12. I wish I had a more confident personality.

我希望我的個性更有自信。

Note ────────────

1. outgoing〔'aʊt,goɪŋ〕 *adj.* 外向的
6. spendthrift〔'spɛnd,θrɪft〕 *n.* 浪費者
7. conspicuously〔kən'spɪkjʊəslɪ〕 *adv.* 引人注目地
9. overhear〔,ovɚ'hɪr〕 *v.* 無意中聽到　moody〔'mudɪ〕 *adj.* 陰沈的；憂鬱的
unpredictable〔,ʌnprɪ'dɪktəbl̩〕 *adj.* 不可預測的

66. What I Believe In
信 念

1. **A**: You don't have any strong political belief, do you?
   你沒有任何强烈的政治信念，有嗎？

   B: Yes, I believe in democracy. I consider that only democracy can ensure that every person is equal in political rights and make the country improve unceasingly.
   有，我信仰民主。我認爲唯有民主才能確保每個人在政治上的平等，並使國家不斷地進步。

2. **A**: What's your attitude toward the work ethic?
   你對工作的道德原則採取什麼態度？

   B: I have a very positive attitude toward work, because it is my work that supports me and my family.
   我對工作的態度很積極，因爲工作養活我和我的家人。

3. **A**: What is your life motto?
   你的生活座右銘是什麼？

   B: Never put off till tomorrow what can be done today. I've found that procrastination makes one feel like he's achieved nothing in life.
   今日事，今日畢。我發覺拖延使人生毫無成就感。

4. I'm not committed to any political party right now.
   我目前不屬於任何政黨。

5. I prefer to wait and see how things go before I make my mind up.
   我喜歡先等一等，看事情進行得怎樣，再作決定。

6. It seems to me that a **human** being has to do more than just work.

　我認爲人除了工作以外，似乎還得做其他的事。

7. I agree with the proverb that fortune and misfortune succeed each other ─ a combination of " Pride comes before a fall, " and " Every cloud has a silver lining. "

　我贊同諺語說的禍福相倚──這是「驕者必敗」和「塞翁失馬焉知非福」的綜合。

8. I believe in always looking on the bright side of things.

　我深信總要看事情好的一面。

9. I'm a big believer in saying what you mean.

　我認爲要言由衷。

10. I don't think it's a good idea to rock the boat more than necessary.

　我認爲非必要的破壞現狀並不是個好主意。

Note ────────────

  1. unceasingly〔ʌn'sisɪŋlɪ〕*adv.* 不斷地

  2. ethic〔'εθɪk〕*n.* 倫理；道德原則

  3. motto〔'mɑto〕*n.* 座右銘　　**10. *rock the boat*** 破壞現狀

67. The Future
將　來

1. **A**: Do you have any ambitions for the future ?
   你對將來有什麼抱負？

   B: One day I'd like to break away and start up a company of my own.
   我將來想離開，自組公司。

2. **A**: How long do you think it will be before you're promoted?
   你想你要多久才會升？

   B: I'm not due for promotion for quite a few years.
   我過幾年也不能升。

3. **A**: What plans do you have for retirement ?
   你有什麼退休計畫？

   B: It's too early to make definite plans, but I'm determined to take things easy.
   現在訂明確的計畫還太早了，但是我決定要過得自在些。

4. I don't think I'll ever get beyond section chief.
   我想我升不到課長以上。

5. I can't see myself as a director.
   我無法想像自己當主管。

6. As long as your family is happy and your income is reasonably good, I don't see promotion as being so important.
   只要你家庭和樂，收入相當不錯，我不認為晉升有那麼重要。

7. One dream of mine is to rise to a position where I can influence company policy and make a real contribution.
　　我的夢想是升到一個能影響公司決策，並能眞正有貢獻的職位。

8. I'd like to see one of my children take over my business.
　　我希望有一個孩子接管我的事業。

9. We're looking forward to when our children are off our hands.
　　我們盼望孩子自立。

10. My son is mad about airplanes, and says he wants to be a pilot when he grows up.
　　我兒子很迷飛機，他說長大後想當飛行員。

11. She's really too young to know, but my daughter says she wants to be a ballet dancer.
　　我女兒還太小，不懂事，但是她說想當芭蕾舞家。

12. You have to be prepared for the worst, so I have taken out a comprehensive insurance policy for the whole family.
　　你必須做最壞的準備，所以我給全家保了各種險。

Note ——————————

1. *break away* 脫離　　*start up* 開始工作
3. *take things easy* 悠然自得
9. *off one's hand* 責任完成　　11. ballet〔'bælɪ, bæ'le〕 *n.* 芭蕾舞
12. comprehensive〔,kɑmprɪ'hɛnsɪv〕 *adj.* 包羅廣泛的

68. Religion
宗 教

1. **A** : What religion are you?
   你信什麼教？

   B : It may sound strange, but I don't have a faith.
   聽起來也許奇怪，但是我沒有信教。

2. **A** : Have you ever taken part in any religious ceremony?
   你有沒有參加過任何宗教儀式？

   B : I've lived in a temple before where I chanted sutras and worshiped Buddha with the recluses there.
   我曾經在廟裏住過，並和裏面的出家人一起誦經拜佛。

3. **A** : Have you ever been to church?
   你有沒有去過教會？

   B : Yes, once a Christian in my class invited me to go.
   有，有一次一個班上的基督徒邀我去。

4. I'm too scientific minded to become religious.
   我太理智了，不可能信教。

5. I make these visits as a kind of custom, not for faith.
   我去那些地方只是一種習慣，不是出於信仰。

6. Most Chinese people look at religious activities in this way.
   中國人對宗教活動的看法多半如此。

7. I think that having a religion is more or less to make up
   for one's inner emptiness.
   我覺得信敎多少是爲了塡補心靈的空虛。

8. I hate those missionaries because they often bother you
   persistently and don't let you go.
   我討厭那些傳敎士，他們經常纏著你不放。

9. Although I'm not religious, I like hymns and church music
   because they bring me inner peace and happiness.
   我雖然不信敎，但是我很喜歡詩歌和宗敎音樂，它們讓我感到平
   安與喜樂。

10. I've always been interested in Zon and if I have the chance
    I want to learn more about it.
    我對禪宗一直感到好奇，有機會我要多研究。

Note ——————————————

　2. chant〔tʃænt, tʃɑnt〕*v.* 詠唱
　sutra〔'sutrə〕*n.*（佛敎、婆羅門敎的）經
　worship〔'wɝʃəp〕*v.* 禮拜　　Buddha〔'budə〕*n.* 佛陀
　3. Christian〔'krɪstʃən〕*n. (adj.)* 基督徒(的)
　4. scientific〔,saɪən'tɪfɪk〕*adj.* 合乎科學的
　8. missionary〔'mɪʃən,ɛrɪ〕*n.* 傳敎士
　9. hymn〔hɪm〕*n.* 讚美詩；聖歌

69. Buddhism
佛 教

1. **A**: I hear you are a vegetarian？聽說你吃素？

   B: That's right.   I'm a Buddhist. 是的，我是個佛教徒。

2. **A**: How did you become acquainted with Buddhism？
   你是怎麼開始接觸佛教的？

   B: When I joined the Buddhist Study Association in my freshman year of college, I began studying the Sutras and took part in many activities.
   我大一參加佛學社團後，就開始研習佛經，參加許多活動。

3. **A**: Which sect do you belong to？ 你是那個宗派？

   B: I have not limited myself to a particular sect. I try out whatever seems good and appropriate for me.
   我沒有限定宗派，只要是好的、適合我的，我就採行。

4. My family is Buddhist so on the first and fifteenth of each lunar month we must offer sacrifices and pray to the gods. 我家信佛，每月初一、十五都要拜拜。

5. I sit in meditation half an hour each day. Sitting in meditation is good for the body and soul because it can put your heart at peace and your mind at ease.
   我每天都打坐半小時,打坐可以使人澄心靜慮,是修身養性的好方法。

6. My grandmother is a very faithful Buddhist and has been a vegetarian for many years.
   我祖母是個虔誠的佛教徒，她吃素已經有好多年了。

7. The Pure Land sect of Buddhism has great influence among the Chinese people.

淨土宗在中國民間的勢力很大。

8. Although Buddhism is often cited as the folk religion of the Chinese people, it is actually mixed together with Taoism and some superstitious beliefs as well.

中國民間的信仰雖常說是信佛，但事實上是和道教及一些迷信混雜在一起。

9. One of my college classmates became a monk after becoming Buddhist.

我一個大學同學信了佛教後就出家了。

10. After reading some books on Buddhism, I feel Buddhist philosophy is quite profound.

我看了一些佛學書籍，覺得佛教的哲理相當深奧。

Note ─────────────

1. vegetarian〔͵vɛdʒə'tɛrɪən〕*n.* 素食者
Buddhist〔'budɪst〕*n.* 佛教徒
2. Buddhism〔'budɪzəm〕*n.* 佛教
sutra〔'sutrə〕*n.*〔佛教〕經（典）
3. sect〔sɛkt〕*n.* 宗派　 ***try out*** 徹底試驗
5. meditation〔͵mɛdə'teʃən〕*n.* 沈思；冥想
7. the Pure Land sect of Buddhism 淨土宗
8. Taoism〔'tauɪzəm , 'dauɪzəm〕*n.* 道教
cite〔saɪt〕*v.* 引用　 folk〔fok〕*n.* 民族
9. monk〔mʌŋk〕*n.* 修道士；僧侶（ ↔ nun〔nʌn〕*n.* 修女；尼姑）
become a monk 〔***nun***〕出家　 10. profound〔prə'faund〕*adj.* 深奧的

70. Christianity
基 督 教

1. **A**: Are there many Christians in Taiwan?

   台灣有許多基督徒嗎？

   B: A lot. Although I'm not sure of the exact number, I know that of all the religious people in Taiwan, Christians are largest in number.

   很多。我雖然不曉得正確的數目，但是我知道在台灣所有的宗教徒中，基督徒佔最大的比例。

2. **A**: Is it true that Catholics worship the Virgin Mary?

   聽說天主教拜聖母是不是？

   B: No, although Catholics deeply respect the Virgin Mary, they have always believed in Jesus Christ.

   不對，天主教雖然尊崇聖母，但仍然信奉耶穌基督。

3. **A**: Have you been baptized?

   你受過洗嗎？

   B: Yes. My baptismal name is Peter.

   受過，我的教名是彼得。

4. My wife is a devout Catholic, and goes to Mass every Sunday.

   我太太是個虔誠的天主教徒，她每個禮拜天都去望彌撒。

5. My children are being brought up as Catholics.

   我的小孩被教育成天主教徒。

6. I regularly do voluntary work for the local church.

我定期替本區的教會做志願工作。

7. More and more people are getting married in church, even though they don't believe in Christ.

愈來愈多人在教堂結婚，即使他們並不信敎。

8. Christmas is celebrated in Taiwan, but most people don't regard it as a purely religious festival.

台灣慶祝聖誕節，但是人們並不把它看成純宗敎性的節日。

9. When I was young I wanted to work as a missionary and spread the Gospel.

我年輕時想做傳敎士傳佈福音。

10. My family's Protestant faith covers all aspects of our daily life.

我家的新教信仰籠罩了日常生活所有的層面。

Note ────────

2. the Virgin Mary 聖母（瑪利亞）
Catholic〔'kæθəlɪk〕*n.* 天主教徒　Catholicism〔kə'θɑlə,sɪzəm〕*n.* 天主教
3. baptize〔bæp'taɪz〕*v.* 爲～施洗
baptismal〔bæp'tɪzml̩〕*adj.* 洗禮的　～ name 洗禮名；教名
4. devout〔dɪ'vaʊt〕*adj.* 虔誠的
Mass〔mæs, mɑs〕*n.* 彌撒　*go to Mass* 望彌撒
9. missionary〔'mɪʃən,ɛrɪ〕*n.* 傳敎士
Gospel〔'gɑspl̩〕*n.* 福音
10. Protestant〔'prɑtɪstənt〕*adj.* 新敎徒的

71. Festivals
節　慶

1. **A :** What special holidays are there in China?
   中國有什麼特別的節日？

   B : First is the Spring Festival of course, then there's the Lantern Festival, Tomb Sweeping Day, etc.
   第一個當然是春節了，再來有元宵節、清明節等等。

2. **A :** Is there anything special about Chinese New Year?
   中國的新年有什麼特別的地方？

   B : I guess eating New Year cake, putting up lucky inscriptions, giving lucky money, lighting firecrackers, wearing new clothes and wishing everyone Happy New Year are all special customs for Chinese New Year.
   我想吃年糕、貼春聯、發壓歲錢、放鞭砲、穿新衣到處拜年等都是中國年特有的習俗。

3. **A :** What type of holiday is the Lantern Festival?
   元宵節是什麼樣的節日？

   B : The Lantern Festival is on the 15th day of the first lunar month. It's the first holiday right after the Spring Festival which also means that the New Year's festivities have come to an end. On this day people eat full-moon dumplings, parade with lanterns, and also hold riddle contests. 元宵節在農曆正月十五，是緊接著春節之後的第一個節日，也表示年節的活動到此告一段落。在這一天人們吃元宵，提燈遊行，並舉辦猜謎大會。

4. April 5th is the Tomb Sweeping Day. Chinese people go to their ancestor's graves to pay their respects, offer sacrifices and do grave-sweeping on that day.

   四月五日是清明節，中國人都在這一天到祖先的墳墓去清掃、祭拜。

5. On the Dragon Boat Festival (the 5th day of the fifth lunar month), we make glutinous rice tamale, and race dragon boats in memory of the patriotic poet, Chu Yuan, who drowned himself in a river.

   我們在端午節（農曆五月五日）包粽子、划龍舟，紀念投江自盡的愛國詩人——屈原。

6. The Mid-Autumn Festival is a holiday on which Chinese people get together to gaze at the moon.

   中秋節是中國人團圓賞月的日子。

7. The seventh month of the lunar year is called "Ghost Month". In the middle of this month, people everywhere set a day to hold a magnificent ceremony in order to release souls from suffering. That day is called the "Ghost Festival".

   農曆七月俗稱"鬼月"，在這個月的中旬，民間各地都會選定一天舉辦盛大的儀式來超渡孤魂，那天就叫"中元節"（鬼節）。

8. It is said that the Cowherd and the Spinster, the stars in heaven, can only meet on the Seventh Eve—— the 7th day of the seventh lunar month, so this day has become the Lover's Day. 據說牛郎、織女星只能在七夕——農曆七月七日相會，所以這天就成了情人節。

9. This year during the Spring Festival I plan to go traveling down south with a few friends.

　　今年春節我打算和幾個朋友南下遊覽。

10. I remember when I was small I always took part in the parades and marched everywhere with my lantern. Once my lantern caught fire due to carelessness. Now when I think back on it, it sure was fun.

　　我記得小時候每逢元宵節一定提著燈籠跟人到處遊行，有一次不小心把花燈燒掉了，現在回想起來眞是有趣。

Note ————————————

1. Spring Festival 春節　lantern〔'læntɚn〕*n.* 燈籠
Lantern Festival 元宵節　Tomb Sweeping Day 清明節
2. New Year 新年　New Year cake 年糕
put up 張貼　inscription〔ɪn'skrɪpʃən〕*n.* 題字
lucky inscriptions 春聯　lucky money 壓歲錢
firecracker〔'faɪr,krækɚ〕*n.* 鞭炮
3. lunar〔'lunɚ〕*adj.* 陰曆的　Lunar New Year 陰曆新年
festivity〔fɛs'tɪvətɪ〕*n.* 歡宴　*pl.* 慶祝活動
full-moon dumplings 元宵　parade〔pə'red〕*v.*（*n.*）遊行
5. Dragon Boat Festival 端午節
glutinous〔'glutɪnəs〕*adj.* 黏的　～rice 糯米
tamale〔tə'malɪ〕*n.* 墨西哥人吃的一種粽子
glutinous rice tamale 粽子　dragon boat 龍舟
in memory of 紀念　Chu Yuan 屈原
6. Mid-Autumn Festival 中秋節
7. release souls from suffering 超渡
Ghost Festival 中元節　8. cowherd〔'kau,hɚd〕*n.* 牧牛者
spinster〔'spɪnstɚ〕*n.* 紡織女　Seventh Eve 七夕

72. Saying Goodbye
說 再 見

1. **A** : Do you have to leave so soon ?

　　你這麼快就得走了嗎？

　B : I'm afraid so ; I have a lot of things to do.

　　恐怕是的；我有好多事要做。

2. **A** : Can't you stay a bit longer ?

　　你不能再待一會兒嗎？

　B : I'm sorry, but I really must go now.

　　抱歉，我眞的得現在走。

3. **A** : It's been a pleasure meeting you.

　　很高興認識你。

　B : The same here ; I'm looking forward to the next time.

　　我也是；盼望下次再見面。

4. Is that the time ? I must hurry.

　是那時候嗎？我得趕快。

5. I must apologize for taking up so much of your time.

　佔用你那麼多時間眞對不起。

6. I'm very grateful for the opportunity to talk to you.

　我非常感謝有機會和你談話。

7. Thank you very much for inviting me; I've really enjoyed myself.

   很感謝你邀請我；我眞的玩得很高興。

8. I can't remember a party where I've enjoyed myself so much.

   我不記得我曾經參加過這麼愉快的聚會。

9. I think our meeting was an extremely fruitful one.

   我認爲我們的會議成果豐碩。

10. I'm so pleased that everybody got along so well together.

    我很高興大家在一起處得那麼好。

11. Please don't bother to see me off.

    請別麻煩給我送行了。

12. Well, goodbye then, and thank you again.

    嗯，那麼再見了，再次謝謝你。

重要美術家名

Botticelli 〔ˌbɑtɪ'tʃɛlɪ〕 波提切利

Cezanne 〔se'zɑn, sɪ'zæn〕 塞尚

da Vinci 〔də 'vɪntʃɪ〕 達文西

Degas 〔də'gɑ〕 德加

Delacroix 〔dəla'krwɑ〕 德拉克羅瓦

El Greco 〔ɛl 'grɛko〕 埃爾・格雷考

Gainsborough 〔'genz,bʒo, -,bʒə〕 根玆博羅

Gauguin 〔ˌgo'gɛ̃〕 高更

Giotto 〔'dʒɔtto〕 喬陶

Goya 〔'gɔjɑ〕 哥雅

Hogarth 〔'hogɑrθ〕 霍加斯

Holbein 〔'hɔlbaɪn, 'hol-〕 霍爾班

Manet 〔mə'ne, mɑ'nɛ〕 馬內

Matisse 〔ˌmɑ'tis〕 馬蒂斯

Michelangelo 〔ˌmaɪkl̩'ændʒə,lo〕 米開蘭基羅

Millet 〔mɪ'le〕 米列

Picasso 〔pɪ'kɑso〕 畢卡索

Raphael 〔'ræfɪəl〕 拉菲爾

Rembrandt 〔'rɛmbrænt〕 林布蘭

Rodin 〔ro'dæn〕 羅丹

Rubens 〔'rubɪnz〕 魯賓斯

Titian 〔'tɪʃən, 'tɪʃɪən〕 提香

Toulouse-Lautrec 〔tu'luz, lo'trɛk〕 土魯斯・羅特列克

Turner 〔'tʒnɚ〕 透納

van Gogh 〔væn 'go〕 梵谷

心靈饗宴

英文自我介紹

作　　　者 / 顏其希	
發　行　所 / 學習出版有限公司	☎ (02) 2704-5525
郵撥帳號 / 05127727-2 學習出版社帳戶	
登　記　證 / 局版台業 2179 號	
印　刷　所 / 裕強彩色印刷有限公司	
台北門市 / 台北市許昌街 10 號 2 F	☎ (02) 2331-4060
台灣總經銷 / 紅螞蟻圖書有限公司	☎ (02) 2795-3656
美國總經銷 / Evergreen Book Store	☎ (818) 2813622
本公司網址 www.learnbook.com.tw	
電子郵件 learnbook@learnbook.com.tw	

書 + MP3 一片售價：新台幣二百八十元正

2013 年 9 月 1 日新修訂

ISBN 978-957-519-982-1